Cindy Ella

A Cinderella Retelling

BLP Fairytales

Denise Essex

B. Love Publications

I dedicate this book to everyone who enjoys black fiction written by black authors!

Acknowledgments

I'd like to acknowledge:

My family: Thank you for allowing me to take up space as an author.

BLP: Thank you for your advice, support, and encouragement.

Editors and proofreaders: Thank you for your patience and all the invaluable information you share!

My accountability partners: Thank you for motivating me with your inspiring goals and holding space for mine!

Me: Thank you for *continuing* to do it, despite your fears. I see you, Goddess!

Readers: Thank you for taking time from your life to play in my world!

Preface

Dear Reader,

Thank you for your interest in my current release. This is a modern take on the fairytale *Cinderella*. If you enjoy what you read, **leave a five-star rating and review on Amazon, and a positive review on Goodreads and TikTok**. Also, be sure to recommend it to your friends. **Follow me on Amazon and** sign up for my mailing and SMS list so we can keep in touch.

Mailing list
    Get steamy texts from your favorite book baes 💋

With Love,
    Denise Essex

Sweet Heat
DENISE ESSEX

Chapter One

"Ella," her father stated with his weathered hands intertwined. He cracked his knuckles as he shuffled into the living room. Cynthia Ella Miller—lovingly known as Ella by her father, Alonzo Miller, and Cindy by her friends—craned her neck so her eyes could follow his entirety as he approached.

Ella studied the gray in his eyebrows that huddled together.

"I need to call you back, Kofi," Cindy sang more than spoke into her cellphone. She bobbed her head in response to his question. "Yep, it's Mr. Miller. I'll tell him you said hello."

"I really like that kid," her father announced as he bent himself and took a seat beside his only daughter on their worn, reupholstered sofa. Her late mother selected the furniture for their home, and neither of them had the heart to part ways with it.

"Daddy." Cindy huffed. She wasn't in the mood for a conversation about how much of a great guy Kofi was. Her father would have to accept that Kofi wasn't her type. If he couldn't make her mouth water, she only wanted to be his friend or flirt with him to pass the time.

Cindy saw Kofi several weeks ago at a party, and he'd asked

around for her number. He finished his internship with the local Paradise Pet Care Hospital where she'd recently applied for an internship. Cindy first met Kofi when they were both undergraduate students.

In the years since, they lost touch and were now both veterinary school graduates. Cindy was impressed to learn that Kofi, who graduated a year before her, was officially Dr. Kofi Carter. There was nothing sexier than a man who cared for animals—because animals were her love language. Although Cindy yearned for her happily ever after, she needed the adrenaline of her prince charming. She didn't get flutters when it came to Kofi.

She quivered when she spoke to her cutty buddy, Dante. Whenever she saw his name on her phone, her thighs clamped together because of what he was capable of.

"The best partners are the ones you're also friends with," Alonzo added, intruding on her thoughts of Dante.

"I get that. But there's no... spark. He's more like a play cousin. Now what has you in knots? I know it's not my friendship with Kofi."

"I could never get much past you. It's about Tremaine and I."

Cindy's stomach lurched. She adored her father's girlfriend. Although they'd only dated for around six months, Cindy was accepted by her and her twin daughters. Because Cindy never got the chance to meet her own mother, who passed away during childbirth, she yearned for an intimate maternal relationship of her own.

Her favorite teachers and mentors were all motherly. Cindy gravitated to women with poise, grace, and elegance. Mama Tremaine, a name she instructed Cindy to call her in place of Ms. Tremaine, was all those things and more. She listened to Cindy intently whenever they spoke and included her in plans she had with her children. She'd even given Cindy the nickname Cindy Ella.

Cindy held her breath, hopeful they hadn't parted ways already. Her dad was a handsome yet sometimes inflexible man. He talked about her mother like they were still an item, and most women chose not to compete with her blameless ghost. Had her father run another potential mate away?

"What about you and Mama Tremaine?" Cindy's lip trembled.

"I want to ask her to marry me. We're older, so early on, we discussed whether either of us would marry again. But she was adamant that I needed to speak with you first whenever the time came." He'd shifted his body to face his daughter while he used his thumb to crack each of his long fingers.

Cindy's eyes closed, and her shoulders fell from the heavens. *Thank God!* The corners of her mouth lifted along with her curvy frame. She stood in front of the couch, aware of her father's apprehension—it was written all over his face.

Cindy's arms flew in the air, and she swung her knees in her favorite happy dance. "Yes! Yes! Yasssssss!"

Alonzo Miller stood with water in his kind eyes and lifted his daughter, swinging her in a circle.

* * *

"Did you tell them to seat you on the balcony? It's much more romantic there." Cindy fiddled with her father's tie, three and a half arduous weeks after he asked her permission to propose. Mama Tremaine had to get onboard. The world would crumble around Cindy if she didn't.

"Yes, for the umpteenth time. You're making me crazy, girl." Alonzo slipped the tie from his daughter's shaky hands and stepped around her to view his reflection in the full-length mirror.

The proposal was to take place in less than an hour. Time moved at the pace of a snail as Cindy anticipated her future stepmother's response. Mama Tremaine would be her bonus mom because Cindy manifested her. For years, she watched her friends with their mothers —they had given her a living, breathing vision board. Although it took longer than Cindy hoped, her dreams had come true.

"You sure I can't watch from the car?"

Alonzo tightened his tie one last time, then turned to take her nose between his pointer and middle finger. "Ella?"

"Yeah?"

"I'll tell you all about it when I get home." He loosened his fingers from her face to grab the sides of her ginger-hued cheeks between his reassuring hands. "It's going to be fine." Alonzo pushed away strands from her cherry-colored ponytail and planted a kiss on Cindy's forehead.

He strolled toward the door dressed impeccably. There was no way he'd be rejected in his navy tailored suit that made him appear a decade younger than he was. From the doorframe of the bedroom, he said, "Don't wait up."

Cindy blushed. Her father and Mama Tremaine should make love and have a late in life baby as far as she was concerned. The more siblings she had, the happier she'd be. She stood motionless as her father left the room and eventually the house. Her body swayed from side to side as she hummed, "So this is love."

Cindy couldn't wait to celebrate. Everything in her room needed to be perfect when her father brought Mama Tremaine to the house to share their good news. She sauntered to her room and picked up several pairs of her favorite sneakers from her hardwood floor. She stuffed them with paper to maintain their proper shape and arranged them neatly in the tempered glass display shelf her father assembled for her. She'd already sprayed it down this week which made her shoes look fit for a princess.

Maybe Cindy and her sisters would wear each other's shoes. Now she would know what it was like to borrow clothes from a sibling—it was something she envied in her friends who had older sisters. Butterflies fluttered around in her stomach as she spun and belted the song that spoke to her as a child, "I'm all aglow, mm." Cindy wouldn't make it through the evening without heading to the restaurant, where her dad made reservations for himself and Mama Tremaine, to watch and record the best day of her life.

Her father's happiness was everything to her. His romantic love and good news also meant the answer to her prayers. She would be part of the loving family she fantasized about. If she was to be on her best behavior and give them the privacy they deserved, she needed to occupy her time elsewhere. The fall homecoming afterparty started thirty minutes ago. It would be the perfect distraction.

Dr. Kofi Carter slid into her private messages on social media. He'd shared the party's flier and simply wrote, 'hope I see you here'. She sashayed her wide hips into her closet door with a giggle. Cindy was graceful in her heart, but most times she could be found bumping into objects that were large and stationary. Her father insisted her clumsy nature was part of her charm.

She pulled out a pair of chocolate-colored joggers that were baggy, yet still hugged her hips and ass wonderfully. She paired it with an oversized dark brown hoodie that exposed her toned belly. Cindy had a custom pair of brown sneakers that matched her outfit to a T. The shoes were high tops, and the sole of the shoes featured a white platform that made her taller than she already was and exaggerated her stallion silhouette.

Fall was the time of year that Cindy let her inner tomboy free. She adored her fitted dresses and girly accessories in the spring, but for now, she opted for sweatshirts and sweatpants.

The October party was to be held in an exclusive location between the all-girls Gullah College she attended for undergraduate school and the all-boys Geechee College. Kofi went to Geechee. Seeing him recently had thrown her off a bit. He was a decent man, and that seemed to be the most important quality to her father. But for her, she wanted to be enthralled.

Cindy's heart beat for a man who could sweep her off her feet. If Kofi had stepped up and shot his shot in college, maybe she would have given him a chance. At twenty-four years old, she needed the type of sparks her dad and Mama Tremaine had if she wanted to get started having kids.

As she stepped into the shower, unbothered at how late she would arrive at the party, she meditated on the names she picked out for her daughters. Cindy continued to hum and lather her skin with her confidence body wash. She charged every product she purchased with a positive affirmation. The soap she showered with was to release any body image issues she had.

No matter how down she was about the last twenty pounds she wanted to lose, her showers lifted her spirits, so she went into the world with her head high and her aura clean. Cindy used her after shower oils that she labeled as magnetism. The affirmation she used for it was that she would attract people and situations that were for her highest good when she wore it. Tonight, she wanted to mesmerize a man whose swag matched hers.

She used her hot pink detangling brush to comb her fire red hair into a high ponytail atop her head. The color finally grew on her. When she dyed it a few months ago, she burst into tears the moment her beautician handed her a mirror because it reminded her of the clown from the popular kid's meals.

She covered it for weeks until there wasn't a clean head wrap left in her collection. Cindy acted as though she'd intentionally chosen that shade of red and owned it—she had yet to look back. The miniature purr of Gus interrupted Cindy's daydream. He only required her attention when she was on her way out of the house.

Gus was a Burmese cat. Cindy found him near a dumpster at her school, and he'd been hers ever since. He scurried away when she attempted to pick him up.

"You better be glad I found you. I picked out the name Gus for a mouse. You hear me, Gus? You were almost a mouse."

Cindy originally wanted a pet mouse. People were awful to mice, and they could be pets like any other animal. Why should they be relegated to meals for others? Her father would've eventually caved because she could wear him down, but the same week they visited the pet store was when she found Gus at the rear of her school.

"Don't wait up. Mama might get lucky too!" She puckered her lips in his direction and gave herself a final once over. Her lips blew air, creating a beatboxing rhythm. Between her bassline, she continued her song. "So, this is love. Mmhm." She twerked as she grabbed her bag, keys, and cellphone en route to the homecoming after party.

A similar melody intertwined with a monstrous bass filled the speakers in her sporty coupe. Cindy and her father lived around thirty minutes from her alma mater, Gullah College. As she zipped past Geechee, her mind drifted to thoughts of Kofi. He was easy on the eyes. Maybe an innocent game of cat and mouse would make this party worth it.

Cindy lowered her music as she parked her car in the gravel of the entryway to the homecoming festivities. She took her time as she swung both feet out of the car, then lifted herself like the ladies did in the movies. Most of what Cindy learned about womanhood was self-taught. As a child, she recalled an older woman say how tacky it was to swing one leg out of the car and waddle out with little regard to one's appearance. From that day forward, Cindy swung her legs simultaneously whether she wore a dress or sweats.

The party was in a heavily wooded area. The smell of pine relaxed her, and the chill in the air was a welcomed reminder of her favorite time of the year, fall. She'd been to this cabin numerous times as an undergraduate and a few times during vet school. Most of Cindy's friends were men. She blew out a breath of relief when she recognized Allen.

"Oh, shit. Is that Cynthia Miller?"

She curtsied in response to her government name.

"Still as weird as I remember. You still sing to birds and shit?" Allen's smile was bright as he regarded her.

"I was a vet tech, about to be a veterinarian. I speak bird, Allen. Respect my gift, man."

He pulled her in for an embrace once she reached the top of the steps where he stood. A group of girls on their way out squinted their eyes and kissed their teeth as they passed by. Cindy didn't recognize any of them, so she paid them no mind.

"Dante asked me if you were here like twice."

Cindy averted her eyes. Allen always looked out for her in school because he insisted she trusted too easily. Like her father, Allen wanted a nice guy for her. They would have to get over it. Why settle for nice when she could get her back broken?

A snicker escaped her lips. Dante could certainly get the job done.

"Cindy, baby?" Dante's rasp echoed over the music.

Dante was dark and handsome. He wasn't necessarily short at five feet eight inches tall, but he compensated for his lack of height with unadulterated confidence. There was an edge to him that was beyond words. It was the fierce way he walked and didn't ask for anyone's approval that caught Cindy's eye.

Cindy stood on tiptoes and wrapped her arms around his neck to greet him. Dante took it as an invitation to lift her and walk her into the party. A small lake pooled between her legs at the way he handled her. The lights inside were dim, and the record playing was slow and sensual.

The kitchen's open concept allowed for a bar setup. There was a catering company who supplied the food, drinks, and a bartender of sorts, though some of the alumni helped themselves. Cindy's breath caught when her eyes connected with Kofi Carter... *Dr.* Kofi Carter.

He was perched on a barstool with a beautiful girl practically in his lap. Kofi wasn't into thirsty behavior. His disinterest was loud, although the young lady couldn't hear it. He was in a full conversation with another girl Cindy didn't recognize. They were much more familiar.

Before she could say anything, by way of a hello, Dante pulled her to the center of the living room where other couples danced. Thank God she was in sweats, because if they played any of her songs, Cindy wanted to be free to unrestrictedly move her body.

The music shifted to an up-tempo track that Cindy loved. Her hips swayed, and her body bounced. She took up space, unfazed by the side eyes from the other girls. Besides, she couldn't be held responsible for their men's wandering eyes.

She also couldn't keep her gaze from drifting back in Kofi's direction. He'd cut his hair off, and bald suited him. The pool between her legs that Dante was responsible for, had been accompanied by new thumps of interest, thanks to Dr. Kofi.

She lifted and dropped her ass in time with the music. Both men were in a trance as they watched. Cindy had no shame that she fed two birds with one piece of bread. She dared not kill two birds with one stone, an expression that made no sense to her. Who, in their right mind, would want to kill a bird?

Dante's hands grasped her waist, while Kofi's eyes undressed her. The attention fueled her teasing. She whipped her ponytail around and grinded her waist against Dante's. The song ended, and he whispered that he needed a drink. Her flirtatious grin was her only response.

She hung back but couldn't find anyone else she recognized. Cindy wasn't new to the ways to get a man's attention. She walked slowly in Kofi's general direction to get a drink of her own. While she spoke to the bartender, she leaned over the bar to rest her chin on her hands and arched her back. The heat from Kofi's body was behind her in no time.

"Why you teasin' me?"

She lifted her eyes to meet his elevated height, and her lashes fluttered when she did. But she didn't bother standing from her bent over position.

"Hey, Kofi."

"Don't 'hey, Kofi' me. You were dancing with Dante, but you were doing all that extra shit for me."

Kofi peered down and allowed his eyes to survey her body. It turned her on. His clenched jaw made the pool between her legs morph into a tsunami.

He leaned down to whisper in her ear. "You gonna dance with me?"

As fine as he was, he was still too nice. Kofi asked for permission, but Cindy preferred a man who did as he pleased then asked for forgiveness. She shrugged her shoulders in a noncommittal way.

Kofi continued to grind his teeth. He used his hands to slap her backside—only the way he slapped her connected more with kitty than ass. It hadn't been an accident.

He grabbed her hand and led her back to the dance floor. Cindy's body moved in tandem with the music. The sexiest part of the dance was that Kofi just stood and watched her. He never did a two-step or shifted his gaze to see if anyone found his behavior odd.

Cindy's lips parted as she put in work. She spun and pressed her backside against Kofi's jeans, but he simply held his fist over his mouth and took her in. He may not have moved, but the area between his legs did. Cindy's skin perspired as she let herself get lost in the song and the object of her seduction. She reached her hand behind her and wrapped it around his neck while she continued to grind her ass on his manhood.

She pulled his head down to the side of her face and asked, "Do you have a girlfriend?"

"Thought we was friends."

Cindy muffled her moan and hoped he didn't pick up on it. "We are friends."

Kofi still hadn't moved as she danced against him. "Why are you asking me if I have a girlfriend? You interested in the position?" His lips brushed against her ear when he spoke.

She shifted to face him and regained her composure.

"Are you using me to make that girl jealous?"

Kofi's head craned in the direction where Cindy pointed. "You mean the same way you used Dante to get my attention?"

He had a point there.

"That's not my girlfriend; that's my cousin, Felicia."

Cindy lifted her head to fully face him and lowered her lids as she spoke. "So, she won't mind if I kiss you?" Men lied about stuff like that all the time. *Cousin my ass!*

Kofi dipped his head and pulled her thick lips into his for a kiss.

His hands pulled her hips into him to subtract any remaining space between them. Cindy had never experienced a kiss like the one she shared with Kofi. It wasn't too much, but it damn sure wasn't too little. It gave grown man and somehow frightened her more than the 'tongue her down' kisses Dante was on.

She pulled away in search of where Dante had gone, but Kofi's long arms drew her back in. "I wasn't finished."

She relaxed into his kiss as her earlier song rang through her ears. 'So this is love.' *Shit! Kofi's my friend.*

That time when she pulled away, he let her. She glanced up in time to see him adjust his jeans and wipe his hand across his mouth and untamed beard. He hesitated, but it wasn't her job to tell him he had a chance if he stepped up. He was a whole ass doctor. If he couldn't tell she needed to be convinced, it was his loss.

Cindy resumed her place at the bar and positioned her body so that her elbows rested on the island behind her while she faced the dance floor they'd just abandoned. Kofi leaned against the bar beside her, and for a while, he said nothing.

"I start my internship at Paradise Pet Care at the end of summer."

"No, shit?"

She gazed up to see his chipped-tooth smile. One of his two front teeth was slightly shorter than the other, yet it didn't diminish his attractiveness whatsoever. In fact, it added to his appeal. There was something about Kofi that was familiar to Cindy on a cellular level. She didn't *have* to play games with him, but she wanted to.

"Last time we spoke, you mentioned that's where you did yours, and it turned into one of your first offers."

"You're gonna be my intern?" Kofi's voice was suggestive, and Cindy hadn't missed it.

"Not *your* intern; everybody's." Her smile was wide when she looked up at him.

"Word?"

"I'm hungry." Cindy had a habit of saying exactly what she wanted. She wasn't shy to eat around attractive men when she was hungry, like other women. She wouldn't eat at the party, but her hunger pangs would probably be the reason she left early.

"Me too."

Kofi wanted to eat something, but it sure as hell wasn't food. Her eyes closed briefly as his words enveloped her.

"Let me have you, Cindy."

She stared in his direction but said nothing.

"When I eat, I always clean my plate," he continued.

"Huh?"

"You heard me. Let me have you, friend."

He nodded his head toward the back of the cabin and strolled in that direction. The thump between her legs beat double time as she watched his large frame disappear into the darkness.

"Girl, go before one of these other thirsty heffas does." Kofi's cousin Felicia smiled brightly at Cindy as she threw her head in his direction.

Cindy scrunched her face while she weighed her options. If she went, they could have wild, no-strings attached sex while the home-coming party carried on. But if she stayed, the kitty between her legs might reach up and choke the shit out of her. The monster between his legs brushed against her when she danced on him.

Cindy lifted and winked at Felicia. She did one last survey of the room to see if she could find Dante, but he was nowhere to be found. Other than Allen, she didn't recognize anyone else. Alumni parties included graduates from as early as last year up to whatever year the older man her father's age had graduated. The seasoned gentleman with the salt and pepper beard was attractive, and Felicia sauntered toward him.

The wooden walled hallway stretched several rooms back. Some of the doors were ajar, while others were shut. Cindy's mouth watered at the prospect of what went on behind those doors. Curiosity caused her to reach for one, but Kofi cleared his throat from two doors down. She waved him to come over, and he did.

"You nosy as hell." He lowered his voice, although the music likely muted the volume of their conversation.

Cindy shrugged her shoulders and slowly turned the knob. Her eyes doubled in size, and her hand clapped over her mouth. Kofi was kind enough to apologize and close the door for her because Cindy couldn't move.

"What the hell?" she asked as she stood cemented in place.

"Looks like a hell of a threesome." Kofi grasped her by the waist and grinned down at her.

She would never share the man she was with, but she could get into watching. There was a girl tasting another girl from beneath her, while the first girl swallowed a well-endowed gentleman. Cindy's cheeks tinted. She wouldn't consider herself inexperienced but maybe a bit old-fashioned. Once the doors closed, she relaxed and followed the object of her obscene desires. She was up to eat or be eaten.

Kofi led her into a room and closed the door behind them. The walls were formed with logs. The cozy cabin added to the sensual energy between them. The crackle of the fireplace tickled her ears. Kofi's gaze locked on hers, and he had a wordless conversation with her.

Why doesn't he tell me what he wants? He grabbed her hips and lifted her before she had time to prepare. He set her on the oversized dresser, and one of her sneakers fell in the process. Kofi kneeled and removed the other one without breaking eye contact.

"I told you I was hungry."

Her breath caught. "Yeah."

Kofi removed each of her socks and shimmied her sweatpants over her legs. The cold temperature of the surface against her thighs brought a welcomed chill. He pulled her to the edge of the dresser and swept her thin panties to the side as he placed his face between her legs. Cindy's moan was loud and tortured. She threw her head back and relished his lips on her sensitive flesh.

His rough hands encircled her cheeks while his nails dug into her ass. The slurping sounds that escaped Kofi's lips while he feasted on her yoni had Cindy in ecstasy. She couldn't be sure because her eyes were closed, but she could have sworn Kofi used the back of his tongue to beat against her clit. Fuck a flower toy; every girl needed a Kofi between their legs.

Cindy sat in an ocean of her own juices. They multiplied under his sensual assault. He blew cold air from his lips against her but quickly followed it up with warmth, in the way a person fogged up a window. The contradictory temperatures had her on the verge of an orgasm.

A light, melodic chime rang out from her phone. It was a text message notification. Kofi's gaze rose to meet Cindy's eyes.

"I don't wanna stop," she whined.

"Good. But I can't get to you like I want." He lifted her again and gently placed her in the center of the bed. He stared at her but said nothing. She was eye level with the hardened monster that was on her ass earlier. To see it was an entirely different experience, and it was still beneath his pants.

Cindy lifted with only her midriff hoodie and bra on—she was naked from the waist down. "What's wrong?"

"I been waiting for this for a long ass time."

He approached the bed then used his hands to play in her treasure while he maintained the eye contact that made her knees weak.

"You got protection?" she asked as she rested on her elbows.

His eyebrows flew to the heavens, and a growl escaped his lips. "Uh, yeah. I mean, hell yeah, I do." Kofi lifted his body and dug into the pocket of his jeans as Cindy's phone chimed again. They were just text messages. If it didn't ring, she wouldn't stop.

He retrieved a condom, tossed it next to her, then removed his jeans. *Oh, my gawd. He's comin' in a Honda.* His beautiful penis had her speaking gibberish.

He was back in the bed by the time she'd lifted her hoodie over her head. He kissed her, and the taste of her essence on his lips caused a gush between her legs.

"You got wetter. Shit!"

He easily unfastened her bra, and she saw pure delight in his eyes when they connected with her hardened nipples. She responded to his pace and lead. Finally, Kofi didn't ask. He took charge. She wanted him as bad as he wanted her.

He grabbed the condom just as her phone rang with her father's ringtone. 'Ella ella eh eh eh.'

He stilled. "Your dad calls you Ella, right? Is that him?" Kofi's words were tortured and barely above a breathy whisper.

Cindy's shoulders sank. It was him, and she would answer.

"I'm sorry, Kofi."

Chapter Two

The car ride home was quiet, which was normal for Kofi but uncommon for Felicia who spoke more words than he could process per minute. He didn't want to talk about shit. The air around him was heavy, and he needed a cold shower immediately.

"I take it you didn't close the deal with the princess," she said with her face buried in her phone.

"Her name is Cindy." Kofi kept his eyes on the road and sped as much as he could without getting pulled over.

"Like I said, princess."

"Her dad called."

Felicia lifted her head which sent her full, honey-colored 'fro bouncing. He could recognize her hair in a crowd full of people.

It was unnerving to have her eyes bore into the side of his head, so he continued. "He proposed to his girlfriend, and I guess she was supposed to go celebrate."

"You sure?"

"Whatchu mean am I sure? Her dad was loud enough for the whole damn cabin to hear. 'She said yes, Ella. Let's celebrate!'" Kofi gave an offbeat impression of what her father said through Cindy's cellphone.

"Are you sure she wanted to go?"

Kofi's head spun. *She* said *she wanted to go.*

"Just because she said her dad needed her didn't mean she didn't want you to insist y'all finish whatever the hell you started that has you all wound up."

"Fuck!" Kofi punched the center console where his elbow had been. Why the hell couldn't women say what they wanted? How was he supposed to know she said one thing with her mouth but meant another? Tests from a woman were harder than any vet school exam he'd ever taken. If he blew another chance with Cindy, he would punch himself in the balls.

"I'm supposed to make her ignore her old man?"

Kofi adjusted his large frame in the driver's seat. His mid-sized vehicle couldn't hold him properly—the seat was damn near leaned into the back. The first big purchase he would make when his doctor checks rolled in would be a SUV.

Felicia rolled her eyes upward. "This is different from forcing if that's what you're thinking."

"What I'm thinking is why didn't she just say that she could meet up with him later. How the fuck am I supposed to know I have the green light if she picks up the phone while we foolin' around, then explains she has to go?"

"Look, cuz. You're dealing with a real-life princess. I guarantee she watches romantic comedies and reads smutty books. She wants you to sweep her off her feet."

"The fuck?" Kofi's eyebrow shot upward.

The walls of the car closed in on him, and his head throbbed. If only he'd known. Kofi pulled into the driveway of his favorite auntie and uncle's home.

"It's early. You wanna stay?" Felicia asked as she lifted from the passenger side.

"Nah. Tomorrow's October fourteenth—my last day before work."

"You been working there. What's the difference?"

"I was an intern before, and now I'm a doctor."

Felicia chuckled. "Good luck with that and with the princess."

She slammed the door before Kofi could remind Felicia her name was Cindy. He backed out of the driveway with the scent of Cindy's hair still in his nose. He lifted his hand to his face and smelled her treasure. His eyes were closed until a car's horn blared from the lane he'd swerved into. It was cruel and unusual punishment how close he'd come to sealing the deal.

The taste of her remained on his tongue. Would he get a third chance? She'd put him in the friend zone in college because he took things too slow with her. He regretted not making a move.

His cellphone rang, and he almost wrecked his car again when he tried to snatch it from his pants. It wasn't Cindy, it was his ex. He powered his phone off and prayed he didn't miss a call or text from Cynthia Miller.

* * *

Paradise Pet Care was home for Kofi. He was in his element when he was entrusted with a fur family member. Every day, he learned something new, and he couldn't recall a dull day on the job. His scrubs and sneakers were clean, although they wouldn't stay that way. Before Kofi could concentrate on anything, he required coffee and carbs.

He'd been in a meditative zone as he sipped his caffeine. Would they be slammed, or would the hours drag by? He prayed for the former. The last thing he wanted to do was spend his first official day doing paper or busy work.

"Carter, welcome to the team," Dr. Johns boomed. His extended belly barely fit beneath his white coat. It was his way of setting himself apart from the rest of the team. None of the other staff wore white coats because it made them seem unapproachable to the patient owners. Kofi learned early on that if he put pet mamas and daddies at ease, they'd divulge helpful information that could assist him in a diagnosis quicker than if he relied only on himself.

Kofi sat in the break room with his coffee, confused at the older man's declaration. They'd worked together for years, but now that Kofi was also hired as a veterinarian, in many ways they were on the same level—Dr. Johns hadn't accepted it.

Kofi nodded his head upward in lieu of a response. Johns was threatened by Kofi from the first time Kofi stepped foot in the hospital. He was in vet school when they first met, and the team couldn't figure out what was wrong with a large animal patient. Johns singled Kofi out because he assumed he wouldn't know the proper treatment.

If Johns had taken the time to speak to him like he did the other students, he would have known that Kofi grew up on his family's farm. Kofi had been around animals since before he could walk. Johns was caught off guard when Kofi recited the proper protocol. It didn't make things better when his colleagues openly laughed. Not much had changed because Johns was still on a mission to humble Kofi.

"There's a ninety-day probationary period for all positions here at the hospital."

Kofi stood and tossed his cup into the trash. "You moonlighting with human resources these days, Johns?" Kofi's charmed chip tooth was on display when he gave Dr. Johns a firm pat to the back. "I'm sure you can pick up extra shifts if money is tight."

The pep in his step returned from his original coffee high. It was best not to poke the bear, but he couldn't start out bending to make Johns comfortable. He'd been in this cycle for years with his older brothers, and he'd be damned if he started that on the job.

"Hey, Dr. Carter," the vet assistant sang. Kofi could barely remember her name, but he remembered that ass. She had hips and ass he could see from the front.

She started at Paradise Pet Care during his internship and made it clear, with her overt flirtation, that she was interested. What's her name was probably as good in bed as her body fit in those snug scrubs. It would have been a disaster to hook up with someone who worked where he hoped to become a vet. He was technically a doctor during his internship, but now his bank account would more accurately reflect it.

Another failed attempt to knock Kofi down a notch was when Johns announced he still lived at home while the crew was on site for an assisted calf delivery. Ava, the vet tech, was there. Kofi didn't get a chance to address it, because another doctor who'd taken the time to get to know him said that he wished he'd done it so that he, too, could graduate without any debt.

Johns brushed it off, but Ava's eyes widened. She saw dollar signs and security.

"Ava, right?"

She clutched the center of her chest which drew his eyes to her titties. *Shit!* His mind may have pined after Cindy, but his body was disloyal and still pent up from his failed weekend. Ava was the type of woman who could smell a man's physical interest.

"You forgot me, Dr. Carter?"

Every time she said his name in that sultry tone, his dick jumped.

"No, never that. I'm not good with names, but who could forget you?" Sweat beaded on his brow as she smirked and walked past him.

"Your first patient is in room five."

"Tha-thank you, Ava," he stammered.

Kofi took a deep breath and skimmed the chart for his first patient of the day. He was only slightly nervous about his shift. The reality was that as an intern, he'd been flying solo for months. He'd earned the team's trust, and they barely questioned him about any of his choices. The difference now was his name would be alone on all the cases he signed.

If anything went wrong or if by some chance, someone he worked with took legal action, he would be liable. Kofi was up for the challenge. He blew out a breath and focused on the details of the chart

Ava mentioned. A dog with lethargy and dehydration was the patient's chief complaint.

"Chew Barka, what's goin' on, my friend?" Kofi entered the room to see a distraught middle-aged woman with a nervous young boy who nibbled at his thumbnail.

Felicia swore Kofi should be a cop because of the way he read people. It wasn't always what people said, but what they did. So far, their behavior aligned with concern for their beautiful Labrador Retriever. Based on the information in the chart, Kofi suspected the dog may have gotten ahold of table food. Whether they fed it to him or not had yet to be revealed.

The black Lab angled his head up in Kofi's direction, then settled back on the boy's lap.

"My name is Dr. Carter, but you can call me Kofi. I'll be taking care of you today."

"I'm Claire Atkins, and this is my son, Chase." The woman extended her hand toward the doctor, where he observed a large engagement ring and matching band. *Damn, Mr. Atkins must have bread!*

"Nice to meet you. Is Chew Barka always this chill?"

Chase shook his head. "We call him Barka for short."

"That's a cool name. Who came up with that?" Kofi asked while he washed his hands.

"Me and my dad."

As he donned his exam gloves, Kofi asked, "What's Barka normally like?"

"For one, there's no way he'd sit still in this office under normal circumstances. He has more energy than the entire family combined," Claire responded.

"Okay. Barka's heavy on the toddler energy. Got it."

"Exactly," Chase offered.

"How long has he been like this?"

"We noticed it a few days ago," Claire responded. She'd rubbed her hands up and down her thighs for the twentieth time. If she kept it up, she would start a fire in her lap.

"Did anything out of the ordinary happen at your house this past week? Any other pets around? Any house guests?"

"No, not that I can recall. We had a potluck for my book club... if you want to call it that. We were all pretty much raised the same, so everyone ended up eating what they brought. But Barka wasn't with me. My book club is full of women—he prefers to hang with the guys."

"How about you, Chase? You notice anything out of the ordinary?"

Chase lifted from his seat and paced the floor. Unlike his mother, he wasn't worried; he looked downright guilty. Pet owners were aware of the dangers of feeding dogs human food but gave in when they felt those wet noses, the way parents gave in with sweets to their kids.

"Do you have cancer?"

"Chase!" His mother interjected.

"It's cool. My bald head mean I gotta have cancer?"

Chase loosened and laughed at Kofi's quick comeback. Kids and animals weren't that different. Barka tracked Chase's movements like he was his favorite human. Their connection was apparent.

"Now that we've gotten that out of the way, did you notice Barka in the trash can or eating pizza at a sleepover?"

Chase giggled. "Barka doesn't eat pizza, and he doesn't do sleepovers."

For the first time since he was in the exam room, Claire smiled brightly.

Kofi's phone buzzed, and he saw Cindy's name from the face of his paired watch. He cleared his throat and had a hard time concealing his wide smile during the remainder of the exam.

"Based on what I see and what you stated in the chart about Barka's dehydration and disinterest in eating, my hunch is that he may have gotten ahold of some of your people food."

Claire stood and stopped rubbing her thighs for the first time. Her eyes flew to her son who dropped his head.

"It doesn't matter how Barka got the food. What matters is that it can cause serious problems. We'll get him meds and fluids, but my main concern is that we rule out pancreatitis."

"Could he... could he die?" Chase's immature voice cracked.

"You brought him in at a good time. Let's get him hydrated and take some x-rays to make sure he hasn't swallowed a toy—"

"Barka knows better than to eat a toy!" Chase fussed, as if he were insulted by Kofi's line of questioning.

"That's good to hear. I'm going to touch Barka and give him a quick exam, then I'll send you over for labs."

Everything felt normal during the physical exam, and other than a slightly elevated temperature, he didn't find anything of concern. He washed his hands and told them a tech would be in to escort Chew Barka to his scan. Claire and Chase thanked Kofi for his time, and he promised to give them the results and follow-up care at the end of their visit.

The moment he exited the room, Ava was on his heels.

"How did it go?"

Her perfume tickled his nose, despite the safe distance he kept from her. She was a seductress, and he still didn't want to go there. The clack of her tongue ring against her teeth as she spoke almost made him forget that his phone burned a hole in his scrubs. But nothing Ava had to say could keep him from returning Cindy's text.

"It went well. Chew Barka needs ultrasound and X-ray imaging," he said with his back to her.

He stepped outside of the hospital and checked the screen of his phone.

Cindy Miller: My dad and his girlfriend are getting married in four months.

Kofi: Damn that's fast.

Cindy Miller: lol. They're not getting any younger and they don't want to waste time

Kofi: got it. How was the celebration the other night?

He didn't give a shit about her festivities, but he wanted to bring up how excited he'd been to taste her. His body hardened at the mere thought of it.

Cindy Miller: They kind of left me out

Kofi: Huh?

Cindy Miller: When I got home, I interrupted what looked like a private party

Kofi: Word?

She should have stayed with him.

Cindy Miller: His girlfriend showed me the ring and told me how excited she was. But then my dad said they were headed to her house. He said they'd changed their minds about celebrating.

Kofi couldn't decide if he was more disappointed she'd left when she hadn't had to, or if he was glad she suffered almost as much as he had.

Kofi: You shoulda stayed with me

Her text bubbles appeared and disappeared several times. Maybe he shouldn't push the situation via text.

Kofi: Look, today's my first day. I need to get back inside. Can I link up with you later?

Cindy Miller: uh, okay

Kofi slipped his phone back into his pocket and rubbed his hand across the smooth surface of his head. *Hell yeah!*

* * *

He expelled a breath of relief as he parked his car in his parents' driveway. His first shift as a veterinarian had been successful. Besides the brief run-in with Johns, all went without a hitch. It turned out his Chew Barka patient didn't have pancreatitis, nor had he swallowed a toy. The relief on Claire's and Chase's faces when the test results came back negative was the reason he loved working with animals—he brought the people who loved them joy.

Kofi's family lived on a massive five-acre property. The driveway stretched half a mile then ended in front of their two-story home. He moseyed through the front door, headed for the shower. The smell of his mother's food assaulted his nose and stopped him in his tracks.

"Hey, ma." He leaned down to give her a hug. Despite his frustration with his brothers—who had yet to leave home—his mom made the fact that he still lived at home worth it.

"Kofi, baby, how was your first day?" She shifted her body to focus on her homemade biscuits.

"It was alright."

"I don't know why I expected you to give me a rundown." She laughed from her belly like she didn't have a care in the world.

If it were up to Norma Carter, her three boys and their future families would all live under the same roof. But Kofi had other plans. He told his father, Samuel Carter, when he moved back in during vet school that he'd remain at home until one year after his first full-time position, to help with bills. After that, his older brothers would have to carry their own weight for once.

Kofi's older brothers, Devin and Maurice, were unemployed. How the two of them could be satisfied helping with the farm yet not paying their parents anything for rent or the food they devoured was unfathomable for Kofi.

"Because your baby boy is a mute," Devin said as he plowed into the kitchen.

Kofi exhaled a deep breath. Devin hadn't bothered to wash his ass or his hands before he entered their mother's sanctuary. This was his twenty-seven-year-old middle brother's idea of a harmless greeting. Kofi's defense had always been to ignore him and his mother's other son. Some days it was hard to claim either of them.

"I'm going to wash my hands and shower, Mama." Kofi lifted from the kitchen table. He'd been with patients all day, so he couldn't technically judge his brother's uncleanliness. But unlike Kofi, Devin had been outdoors.

"I'm gonna shower, Mama," his brother mocked.

Still unbothered, Kofi attempted to sidestep his brother who decided it would be funny to put him in a full nelson. He grabbed Kofi and wrapped his arms around the back of his neck. Devin used his hands to push down on Kofi's head, while Kofi's arms were raised uncomfortably in the air like he'd done to him since they were kids. But they weren't kids anymore, and Kofi was no longer the string bean he was in his youth.

One of the first things Kofi learned when he left for college was how to defend himself against his brothers and anyone who dared to take advantage of his laid-back demeanor. He covered Devin's hands, yanked him forward, then popped his body upward. The motion sent Devin flying in the opposite direction.

"Kofi," his mother fussed.

"You ain't all that because you learned a few Muay Thai moves," Devin said as he lifted himself slowly from the floor.

Kofi averted his eyes from his mother while his shoulders slumped. He left the room without explanation. Wasn't a mother supposed to protect her youngest? Instead, Kofi was left with the weight of more than his share of financial responsibility and the burden to choose the high road. He didn't mind carrying his own load, but his brothers took advantage of his income and never contributed anything.

His oldest brother, Maurice, had gone so far as to celebrate Kofi's new position because, in his words, they would finally get new furniture. On top of the adulting he shouldered, he always had to be the bigger person.

He grabbed his things and headed to the tiny bathroom. It was time for Kofi to get his own space. He groaned inwardly. He should have given his brother a piece of his mind. *But what good would that do?*

Kofi stepped out of the cramped shower that was like a spa when he was younger to find his towel missing. If his brothers had gone away to college and experienced these shenanigans in their early twenties, they wouldn't need to do it in their thirties. Kofi was hungry, and he'd already had to lay one of them out. His heart pounded as he covered himself with the pile of his work clothes he'd abandoned to wash himself.

He snatched a towel from the hallway linen closet and ignored his mother's other child on his way to his room. Kofi slammed the door and counted backwards as he did his after-shower routine. His phone alerted him of a message, and he prayed like hell that it was Cindy. It was.

Cindy Miller: Hey Kofi

Kofi: Hey yourself. What time are you available?

Cindy Miller: About that...

Kofi: I know you not tryin' to cancel on me

Cindy Miller: I'm sorry, but something came up

Before Kofi could respond, his door swung open, and his older, smaller brother, Maurice, barged in.

"The fuck, man? Don't you know how to knock?"

Maurice held up Kofi's towel. "I figured this was yours. Devin had it, and you and I both know he ain't washed his ass."

Kofi's head lowered back to his phone. He wouldn't give Maurice a round of applause for confiscating a towel from a man three years *older* than him. Maurice often pretended to be the peacemaker of the family, but when push came to shove, he and Devin had an invisible alliance against their little brother. Besides, all Kofi cared about was getting his face between Cindy's legs again. He was so wrapped up in his text messages that he hadn't heard his brother continue into his bedroom.

As he snatched the phone, Maurice said, "You always thought you were better than us because you went to college."

Kofi craned his neck up because there was no need to stand. Neither of his brothers had been able to overpower him physically for years.

"Because you got a little money in your pocket, you better? Answer me!"

"Don't yell at me," was all Kofi said in response to his brother's demand.

Kofi lifted from his spot on the bed and grabbed for his phone. In a predictable, childish manner, Maurice lifted his hand above his head. It used to drive Kofi nuts when he was little because back then, he was too small to get whatever had been taken from him. They tussled for the phone and as if on cue, his middle brother, Devin, entered for an infantile game of 'keep away'.

They tossed Kofi's cellphone back and forth until it crashed against the hardwood floor.

In a powerful voice that stopped them both in their tracks, Kofi roared, "What the hell is wrong with y'all?"

Devin's and Maurice's shoulders sank. If they all didn't share such strong resemblances, Kofi would bet his last dollar that they weren't related.

"Y'all are supposed to be my big brothers! We're too damn old for this shit. I get home from my first day of work, and I can't fuckin' talk to either of you about it, because all you gonna do is tell me how I think I'm better. Then you break my phone! Who's gonna pay for it, huh?" Kofi was on a roll. He'd bottled up his thoughts for years. But those days were over. "Y'all work for Dad but turn around and eat him out of house and home. You know who gonna pay for it? Me. And I'm probably paying for both of y'all phones too."

"Out!" Norma yelled from the door.

Devin and Maurice scurried out of the room in a way that gave Kofi a serious case of déjà vü. They'd always ganged up on him when they were little. Norma closed the door and pointed at his bed. Kofi sat. He had hoped they were in trouble, but it was obvious her issue was with him.

"What has gotten into you?" she asked barely above a whisper.

"Me?"

"Yes, you."

Kofi looked at his phone with a shattered screen. Was she for real?

"I'm not talking about your phone. Things can be replaced. But the way you spoke to your brothers just now," she paused. "It could take a lifetime for them to heal from."

"Huh?"

Norma rolled his desk chair toward the bed so that she sat across from him. Her wide cheeks lifted for the first time since he'd greeted her in the kitchen.

"You're my baby boy in age and birth order, but you've always been more mature than Devin and Maurice."

"Yeah but—"

"Listen, I was the youngest in my family too. But your aunts were irresponsible. That's just the way it was. Who took care of Grandma when she got sick?"

"You did, Mama."

"Do you remember when your aunts were here for a visit years ago, and you asked if I was the big sister?"

"I do." Kofi flashed her a lopsided grin. He'd been certain his mother's sisters were younger than she was.

"They didn't speak to me for weeks because they convinced themselves I put you up to it. The point is, it's not fair that you can't go to your brothers for help. In most cases, they'll probably come to you. Add to that, you can't say or do certain things without breaking their spirit."

"You right. None of this sounds fair. They broke my phone, but I can't call them out about it. I can't tell the truth, Ma?"

"No. That's not what I mean. With family, you learn to accept what each person is capable of. I'm not talking about abuse. Your brothers will hear from me later tonight. It's never OK for them to hit you or damage your property.

"But when it comes to the amount of money they make, have you considered they might be doing the best they can? Have you considered that might be why they're so threatened by you? This started when you were in middle school. You had a growth spurt, a little mustache, and all the girls liked how mysterious you were."

"That wasn't my real personality, Mama." Kofi rubbed his hands across his smooth head. He'd never told his mother what happened at his best friend, Jason's, slumber party. "I know you remember my best friend, Jason, right?"

"Of course. His little girl is adorable. I saw the two of them at the farmer's market just last week. He told me to tell you congratulations on your new gig."

Kofi told Jason he'd be a vet when they were younger. Jason said it was perfect because he would have someone he knew take care of his dogs.

"He had a slumber party when we were in seventh grade. It was a big deal because it was my first time overnight without Dev or Maurice."

"I remember. Neither of your brothers got any sleep that night. Your father had to threaten them because they kept pacing the floor and begging to call and check on you."

Kofi's head shot up. They never told him. He took a deep breath.

"That night, I couldn't sleep either. I couldn't fall asleep without Dev's snoring." Kofi chuckled as he recalled how horrible his brother's snoring was. It bothered him, but he found it difficult to rest without it. "I got up for water when I heard something outside—"

"Bay. Them biscuits smell like they burnin'," his dad said when he flung the door open.

"Oh no." Norma stood with her hand in the center of her chest.

"How was your first day, son?" his dad asked from the door. No matter how tense a situation, Kofi's father was clueless to the emotional state of anyone in his house. He was a man of many positive qualities, but his ability to see beyond the obvious was trash.

"It was fine, Dad."

Kofi grabbed his wallet and keys. He needed to get a new phone so he could see what was up with Cindy before he lost the nerve to ask her out on a non-friendly, more than sexual date.

Chapter Three

A pile of premier wedding magazines was spread out in front of Cindy, on her living room floor, along with the ten bridal window browsers she had opened on her laptop. Her father didn't know the first thing about how to plan a wedding. Cindy would pick up the slack. Mama Tremaine wasn't the type to be threatened by anyone who took a task off her plate. Besides, if Cindy did too much, she wouldn't be offended if Mama Tremaine told her to fall back.

With her internship scheduled to begin after summer, Cindy could capitalize on an opportunity to live vicariously through her father and his fiancée's nuptials in February. The road to becoming Dr. Miller had been more time consuming than Cindy originally calculated. She spoke animals better than she spoke people, yet vet school had involved much more than intuitively treating animals.

There had been mounds and mounds of useless paperwork. It seemed the field was full of people more afraid of being sued than the care of animals. But it was an essential aspect of the job. She loathed the courses on liability and had almost failed one. Anytime she was tested on her ability to say the 'right thing', she instead gave an honest response.

Cindy refused to dodge an owner's concern. When they practiced mock patient history in school, she was given harsh feedback for divulging whether a patient would or would not die. If a dog had cancer, it would die. It was black and white to her. Wasn't it more harmful to give a patient hope when there was none?

But if she wanted to work in a hospital, she was tasked with also ensuring she and the hospital wouldn't be sued. The only way around those strict guidelines was to open her own practice which would take her further from the family she wanted.

Her future husband awaited her. And their three daughters did too. Cindy had convinced herself she would have three or more children, all of whom would be girls. She dreamed of tea parties and endless games of dress up.

Between the wedding and her side job as a party princess, she could wait another year for her prince charming to sweep her off her feet. She started her business as a party princess performer during undergrad because of her roommate, Lori. Cindy fell in love with her roommate's niece, Amara, the moment they met at family weekend. The five-year-old had star power and captivated the hearts of anyone she met.

Lori was embarrassed when she had to hand deliver a golden envelope to cordially invite Cindy to Amara's sixth birthday party, but Cindy was flattered. They were to dress in full royal attire, and Cindy took the instructions seriously. When she and Lori arrived at the party, Lori's sister informed her that the person they hired for entertainment canceled at the last minute.

Cindy begged to stand in. She naturally fell into character. Everyone was to address the birthday girl as Princess Amara. Time flew by, and everyone at the party was swept up in the make-believe world Cindy created. The parents in attendance asked for her contact information to hire her for their children's birthday parties.

When she found out she could make several hundred dollars for an hour of play, she continued the gig throughout college. Cindy was forced to cut back during vet school, but school ended last winter. With almost a year between school and her internship, she accepted more jobs.

Cindy smiled to herself as she gazed at her newest party gown. It was satin and featured an off the shoulder design with long sleeves and a court train. The children would love this one. It hung against the side door.

Her father parked his truck in the driveway, but she didn't bother to clear the clutter. She was in wedding planner mode.

"What is all this?" Alonzo asked once he joined her in the living room.

"White roses, lilies, and moonflowers for Mama Tremaine's bridal bouquet. And Calla Lilies for the bridesmaids."

"Take a breath, Ella," Alonzo said with eyes full of concern. "You know I appreciate your passion here, but Tremaine and I want something simple. In fact, her exact words were 'the smaller, the better'. She doesn't want a big fuss."

Through pursed lips, Cindy responded, "Of course she does. Everybody says they don't want a fuss because they want to seem humble, but once the day arrives, they're grateful for the opulence."

Alonzo sat on the couch near his only daughter and reached his hand down to lift her from where she sat cross-legged surrounded by her research. Once she was near him, he pulled her into a warm side embrace.

He kissed the top of her head and gently added, "I can't wait to do all of this for your wedding. But Tremaine and I are probably going to the courthouse."

Cindy wiggled out of her father's arms. "Absolutely not!"

"What?"

"No, Daddy. You don't want a big wedding? Fine. But I refuse to let this special occasion take place in a sterile courthouse. Those are for divorces."

Alonzo's eyes crinkled in delight. "Twenty people. Plan a small ceremony that will accommodate twenty people, and I'll let you have your way."

"Forty," Cindy offered.

"Twenty-five or we do it at city hall."

"Deal!" Cindy bounced up and down.

She could've made it magical with fifteen, but he didn't need to know that. Mama Tremaine would become a Miller, and her father would have the companionship he deserved. Cindy would finally have the mother-figure she dreamed of since she was a child.

* * *

This was the fourth house they'd toured, and Cindy could tell her new family was over it. If they found something now, they could spend the holidays together. She wanted nothing more than to use the winter months to bond with her sisters and stepmother before the February ceremony. Dreeyah and Stasia were fraternal twin Scorpios who couldn't be more different. They had an interesting dynamic that Cindy wouldn't quite characterize as warm and fuzzy, but they were close. It was as if they spoke their own language that didn't require words.

Stasia spoke to Cindy the most. She was competitive and into men more than Cindy. While everywhere they went, eyes went to both Cindy and Stasia, Stasia was drawn to any man who paid her no mind—she liked a challenge.

Dreeyah, on the other hand, was calm and calculated. Cindy was glad she hadn't met her in high school and that they were practically family. Otherwise, she could have been the type of bully to make her life miserable. Dreeyah didn't do happily ever after. She rolled her eyes when Stasia and Cindy bonded over celebrity romances. Dreeyah was the epitome of the notion that still waters run deep.

Alonzo's SUV sat him and Mama Tremaine and their three adult children.

"It looks like a castle!" Cindy said as they piled out of the car.

"Here we go." Dreeyah huffed.

Cindy saw Stasia push the back of Dreeyah's head, but it didn't deter her sour mood in any way.

The Tudor-styled home with the dramatic, slanted gable roofs was like a real-life castle.

"This is it, Dad." Cindy slid under her dad's arm and accepted his side embrace.

"We haven't seen the inside yet."

"It doesn't matter. I can feel it."

Mama Tremaine stood near the car engulfed in a hushed phone conversation.

"Want us to wait, bae?"

She gave him a mischievous smile but waved them on.

Alonzo unlocked the estate via the lockbox, and he and the girls entered one of the most beautiful pieces of property Cindy had ever seen. She removed her sneakers and ran the length of the downstairs, shouting about the features as she went.

"Please don't put me in a room near princess sunshine," Dreeyah complained.

"I heard that. They have a primary suite down here, Daddy!" Cindy bounced and pointed like a kid in the candy store.

"She's adorable," Stasia added.

The twins were two years younger than Cindy. They were both in their last years of college, but their life experience had them behave more like big sisters when it came to Cindy. She didn't mind it at all.

Cindy made it to the second level before her father and future stepsisters. Her phone chimed with a text message alert.

Dr. Kofi Carter: Cindy Miller.

*Cindy: Hey, Dr. Carter *wink emoji*

Dr. Kofi Carter: Are you flirting with me Cindy?

Cindy: Maybe

Dr. Kofi Carter: Let me see you

Kofi would have to wait. What she wanted was to see the rest of their house. Because if it was up to her, this was where she and her family would live. It was perfect. At the top of the stairs, a large window with an abundance of natural light allowed her to see Mama Tremaine still alongside her father's car.

Her future stepmom let Cindy help with planning the nuptials, but there was still a lot she had to handle on her own. Those plans required lots of paperwork and phone calls. As she continued her conversation, Cindy recognized the glow on her face and the blush on her cheeks. Mama Tremaine couldn't help her smile whenever she discussed the big day.

The rooms upstairs were massive. Each of the girls could have their own room and bathroom. There was a bonus room in the attic that was carpeted and snug but required a little TLC. It would be a nice place for Gus to hang out when he needed his space. She'd introduced him to the girls, and he wasn't a fan. But Cindy was confident he'd warm up to them eventually.

Dreeyah and Stasia made it upstairs as Cindy's phone rang.

"Hey," Cindy said, unbothered that she accepted the call on speaker phone.

"Hey yourself. I wanna see you."

"He sound thirsty as hell," Dreeyah said and moved around her.

"I got you on speaker, Kofi."

"No, he doesn't. He sounds fine. Who are you?" Stasia swiped the phone from Cindy and brought it near her face.

Cindy shrugged and joined her father in the second primary bathroom. The space was large enough to fit two of the bathrooms in their current home. There was a large clawfoot tub located inside an extended shower that took up one half of the room.

"This is beautiful!"

"We're gonna need one hell of a housecleaner."

"Daddy." Cindy snickered as she swiped him playfully on the arm.

"As long as you, the girls, and Tremaine like it, we'll get it."

"It's alright." Dreeyah had her face in her phone. She looked up briefly, but only to watch her step.

Dreeyah appreciated Cindy's father as a new male presence in her life. She may not have been chummy with Cindy, but she lit up whenever Alonzo entered her space. When Dreeyah walked past him, he stuck his foot out so she almost tripped.

"Very funny," Dreeyah said as she poked Alonzo, who was insanely ticklish.

Her dreams had finally come true. She was on top of the world. Nothing could damper Cindy's mood. Not even a bit of harmless flirting between her boy crazy stepsister and her friend.

"How long have you been working there?" Stasia asked in a syrupy sweet voice.

"Almost two months. Can I speak to Cindy now?"

Stasia faced Cindy with an unreadable expression on her face. Cindy waved her hands and mouthed 'no' in response to Kofi's request. She would have let things go all the way with him at the cabin. The things he did with his mouth had her wide open. But the more time that passed, the more passive he was, and the less interested she became.

"Here she is." Stasia arched her eyebrow with a smirk. "You better talk to this successful, fine, black man before I do," she whisper yelled.

"How do you know he's fine?" Cindy pouted.

"I can hear y'all." Kofi piped up.

A blush covered Cindy's features as she wandered down the stairs and out into the backyard.

"They should get married here!"

"Your dad and your stepmom?"

She'd forgotten he was on the phone. Her brain couldn't do two things at once. If Stasia liked Kofi, she could have him. But would she need to tell her about how he'd face planted between her legs? They were sisters now. Did sisters have to tell each other everything?

She hummed her response toward the phone.

"You sound like you miss me?"

Once again, her body betrayed her, and her center thumped with the steady rhythm of a snare drum at the sound of the inflection in his voice. But Kofi was... Kofi. Right now, she wanted her mind on her new family. Men would always be available. She had yet to experience the shortage other women complained about. They were everywhere.

"I have to go."

"Yeah, you might not miss me, but your puss—"

"Cindy Ella? Is that you?"

Mama Tremaine interrupted Kofi mid-sentence.

"I thought I heard a man back here."

Cindy lifted her phone and pointed.

"Kofi, this is my... this is Mama Tremaine, my dad's girlfriend." Cindy tucked her bottom lip between her teeth as she aimed the speaker toward her. The sonar sound of a video call startled Cindy and increased the blush on her face.

"Really?" Cindy sang into the phone as she accepted the video request.

"Damn you're beautiful. Now aim me at the future Mrs. Miller," Kofi demanded. His dark eyebrows were furrowed, and he looked freshly showered.

"Oh my," Mama Tremaine said with her hand rested against her chest. "Who are you?"

"I'm a friend of your stepdaughter's. Kofi Carter." Cindy could see Kofi rub his hand against his dangerously sexy bald head. Why did he have to request a video call? He tried to melt her resolve, and it worked.

"It's nice to meet you. Are you coming to the wedding?" Mama Tremaine had that glow she'd had on her call a few moments earlier. She looked thoroughly pleased, and Cindy envied her for it. But she wouldn't fret because once she got her family together, Cindy was next. It wouldn't be with Kofi though.

Cindy slid her phone from Mama Tremaine's hands. "Okay, Kofi. As you can see, we're still looking at houses. Can I call you later?"

"Real smooth, Miller. You already got a date?" Kofi asked Cindy.

"No. No, she does not," Mama Tremaine inserted.

Cindy released a nervous breath of air.

Mama Tremaine pursed her lips. "I know you're not bringing that raggedy Dante," she added.

Mama Tremaine hadn't been shy about her thoughts toward Dante. She said Cindy could do much better. Apparently, Kofi was acceptable.

Cindy's eyes bucked, and the crease in Kofi's brow deepened.

Mama Tremaine threw her a coy smile like she hadn't intended for him to hear. "Sorry," she mouthed to Cindy. "Nice meeting you, Kofi," she said as she entered the back door to the property.

"Already got a date, huh?"

Cindy wished he would tell her that she wasn't going to the wedding with Dante, and that *he* would be her plus one.

Instead, he said, "I guess I'll let you get back to your family. Let me see you later."

"I'll think about it."

"It's nothing to think about. You gonna need a break, I can tell. I'm taking you to eat later."

"OK." With a big smile and one last roll of her eyes, Cindy disconnected the phone. If only Kofi knew how far he could get with her if he took the ask for forgiveness over asking for permission approach.

* * *

It was February, and they closed on the home Cindy loved before the holidays, just as she hoped—everyone was nice and settled. Her bedroom was on the second floor with her stepsisters, but she was given the primary with the ensuite bathroom because the twins wanted to be near each other.

"You act like this is your wedding, sis."

Dreeyah and Stasia were always in and out since they all shared beauty products, and Cindy had a hell of a lot more space. Cindy continued with her makeup despite her shaky hand.

"Cindy."

"Huh?" She looked up to see Dreeyah with her hand on her hip.

"Who else is in here?" she sassed.

"Oh, you said sis, so I assumed—"

"We're sisters now too. But like I said, you act like it's your wedding day. You want Stasia to help you with that?"

Tears crowded Cindy's eyes. Dreeyah had referred to her as her sis. She absolutely needed a hand.

"Help with what?" Stasia asked.

Stasia, who was normally shorter than Cindy, walked in fully dressed and in her stiletto heels with her makeup done flawlessly. She towered over Dreeyah and Cindy.

"Wow."

"Damn, Stasia. Now, you actin' like you gettin' married. You tryin' to upstage Mom?" Dreeyah shook her head and left her sisters alone in the bathroom.

"What's wrong, Cindy?" Concern tinted Stasia's cognac-colored skin.

With wet cheeks, Cindy replied, "I'm just really happy."

Stasia walked over to where she stood and pulled her into an embrace. "I'm glad your dad met our mom too."

Cindy gathered herself and allowed Stasia to finish her makeup. The wedding planner Cindy insisted they allow her to hire just for the day, popped her head in and told them they had fifteen minutes, as most guests were already seated. A moment of panic washed over Cindy's face.

"Trust me. I'll have you looking like a young Meg Thee Stallion when I'm done with you."

Stasia didn't lie. She did Cindy's makeup and upgraded her

natural beauty. The floor-length satin dress Cindy wore accentuated her hips. The split showcased her thick, long legs.

Because they'd opted to hold the ceremony in the backyard, exactly how Cindy envisioned it, everyone got dressed in their respective rooms, except for Alonzo, who was booted to the bonus room in the attic. As he made his way down the stairs, he clapped his hands and placed threaded fingers against his lips.

"Ella, you look stunning!"

Cindy curtsied before her father as pure elation raced through her veins. When she lifted, he extended his hand for a dance. She accepted, and they swayed on the carpeted hallway as they'd done so many times in her lifetime. She hummed her favorite song while he spoke.

"I peeked out back."

"And?"

"You were right. Tremaine deserves this. It's much better than the court."

Cindy smirked up at him.

"You kept the guest list small like I asked. But..."

"But, what?" Cindy stopped her movement.

"I added two."

Cindy shrugged her shoulders and resumed their dance.

"Y'all are weird as hell," Dreeyah said as she shuffled past them. Although she was a petite young girl with delicate features, her personality was as flat and sarcastic as a bartender with a smoker's cough. She was the culmination of unbothered and, in that way, the exact opposite of Cindy.

Alonzo threw his leg up behind him and gave her a tap to the rear. With a chuckle, she repeated, "See. Weird."

"Who'd you invite, Daddy?"

"My guy, Kofi."

Cindy's eyes widened. They never got around to dinner the night she and the family toured the home. Had Kofi brought a date to her father's wedding? It shouldn't matter. He wasn't her man, but still.

"He insisted you would let us both have it if I selected him as your date, so he asked if he could bring his cousin. Somebody named Felicia. And don't worry. I told him exactly what I'd do if this was some play cousin he has sex with."

"Daddy!"

"Daddy, nothing. I don't like him that much."

Cindy used her fingers to smooth the scowl from her father's face. "I love you."

"I love you more, Ella."

"I'm sorry to interrupt such a beautiful moment," the wedding planner said with a mist in her eyes. "But, Mr. Miller, it's time for you to take your place outside."

Beside the wedding planner was a stealthy wedding photographer who'd taken several pictures from his knees on the carpet. Alonzo leaned down and kissed Cindy on her forehead then released her. She found her sisters and caught a glimpse of her bonus mom. Mama Tremaine was breathtaking, more than Cindy could have dreamed for her father.

She wore a cream-colored vintage wedding dress that was styled like it was the 1940s. The V-neck garment was fitted at the top with a tea length that added to her graceful yet sensual appearance. Outside, the mixture of small and large string lights made the festivities look like they took place under a sky full of stars. The outdoor heaters ensured that guests would be comfortable in their wedding attire.

The decor was a play for play replica of the original vision Cindy had for her father's wedding, only scaled down three times. She smirked as she stood at her father's side across from Mama Tremaine and her twin sisters. While the pastor spoke about marriage, Kofi's eyes raked across her silk dress. Her body responded, and she prayed no one else noticed.

Fine wasn't a strong enough word to describe how he looked in his suit. He'd dressed up for the occasion and hadn't torn his gaze from her since she stepped into the backyard. She bit her lip and willed herself to pay attention. Each time she focused on her father and his bride, Kofi undressed her with his eyes. The worst part was she didn't mind.

He'd come with Felicia, who had a similar nonchalant demeanor like Dreeyah. It was clear who the "wedding" people were and who'd attended to appease someone else. Her large blonde 'fro caught the attention of her dad's youngest brother, David. Cindy internally gagged. Although Uncle David was younger than her father, he was still in his early forties.

Mama Tremaine and her father's vows were brief. They spoke about how blessed they were to find love again. Alonzo made a point to include his love for his two new daughters and how relieved he was that their families had already blended so well. He promised to give his life for any of the four loves of his life, and that was when Cindy could no longer hold back her tears.

"I now pronounce you Mr. and Mrs. Alonzo Miller."

Alonzo kissed Mama Tremaine passionately. Dreeyah looked away, but Cindy secretly hoped she might get another sibling. When her eyes drifted to Stasia, she caught her staring... at Kofi. *Shit!*

The wedding party table consisted of the new Miller family. So far, Dreeyah and Stasia had both done toasts. Cindy stood on wobbly legs, prepared to give hers.

"For my whole life, it's just been me and my dad."

"Aye," Uncle David cut in, garnering laughs from the rest of the guests.

"Right. For my whole life, it's just been me and my dad *and* Uncle David. And Auntie Sheryl, and Aunt Roshelle, and Auntie Belinda—"

"That's enough," Uncle David said flatly.

"I love you, Uncle David."

As the laughter died down, Cindy continued. "I watched my dad mourn my mom for years. Even though I never got the chance to meet her, I knew she must have been amazing. As I grew up, I wanted nothing more than for my dad to love again. Then he met Mama Tremaine." Cindy dabbed at her eyes. "You've changed my dad in ways you'll never know. He's always been a kind and present father. But separate from his roles and obligations, he's never been happier as a man. Thank you, Mama Tremaine, for loving him past his flaws and making space for us both in your life."

"Cindy Ella." Mama Tremaine stood and pulled Cindy into a warm hug. They were joined by her father and Stasia who reached over and pulled Dreeyah to them. More laughter from the other guests kept Cindy from being overtaken with emotion. Finally, she was complete.

Dinner was served, and Cindy was famished. She hadn't eaten a full meal since the previous day. Every now and again, she would peek in Kofi's direction. He was more good-looking than she remembered.

Her cellphone rumbled in her sleek purse. Between generous mouthfuls, she retrieved it, curious about who'd messaged her.

Dr. Kofi Carter: You lookin' at me

Cindy Miller: So what? I'm looking at everyone here

Cindy smirked while she quickly typed messages behind the long fabric of the table. With his new demanding job and her big move, they hadn't spoken much.

Dr. Kofi Carter: Nah. You givin' me that look

Cindy Miller: This look?

She scanned him and his long, muscular legs. They were opened. Would he get a second chance to use the hardware that rested between them? She had no doubt that the intention in her stare was obvious to both Kofi and anyone else who faced her direction. Cindy giggled when Kofi pulled at his tie. Her smile faded when he stood.

Panicked over what he might pull, she typed another quick message.

Cindy Miller: I'm joking. What are you doing?

His phone dinged, but it only slowed his gait momentarily. In no time, he was before the head table face to face with Cindy and her family.

Alonzo reached out his hand to him. "Glad you could join us, Kofi."

"Congratulations, Mr. Miller. You're a very lucky man." His eyes shifted from Alonzo's to Tremaine.

"Thank you," she responded. "He's much more handsome in person," she whispered to the girls.

"He sure is," Stasia muttered.

With a sheepish grin, Kofi thanked Mama Tremaine and reached for Cindy.

"What are you doing?" Cindy liked Kofi, but they were friends. There was no need for him to be this intimate while other people outside of the family could see.

"We're dancing."

Cindy stood and followed him, mainly for the purpose of getting some distance between her unpredictable libido and her father. He assisted her down the few steps of the lifted platform where she and the others sat while he watched her intently.

"But the DJ hasn't started."

"We don't need any music."

"I know that's right," Mama Tremaine said behind them.

The dance floor was clear which gave the illusion the two of them were floating. Kofi pulled her snug against him, and Cindy's breath caught in her throat. Who was this Kofi, and what had he done to the unmotivated guy from undergrad?

Kofi was handsome, just too passive for her liking. Whatever Wheaties he'd eaten had not only done him well physically but had pushed him to direct her in the way her body preferred.

"You forgot about the night your pops proposed?"

His warm breath was near her ear, and the sensation sent shivers of satisfaction down the exposed skin of her back.

"How could I?"

He leaned back to stare into her face. Now he was giving her the look.

"It was a big night for them," she added. She hoped her words sounded as convincing to him as she wanted them to.

"I'm talking about what happened to you right before you got the call."

Her breath hitched.

"You was lookin' at me like you wanted more of that."

She most certainly did. Her mouth opened, but she couldn't decide what to say.

"Mind if I cut in?"

Dante's timing couldn't have been worse.

"What are you doing here?" she asked on an exhale. Kofi's embrace had caused her to forget where she was.

"I saw the video you posted on social media and thought I'd slide through. I know how much you like this romantic shit." Dante's voice was harsh. He couldn't care less where he was; he didn't adjust his rough demeanor to suit the environment.

"Do you mind?" Cindy searched Kofi's eyes. Her heart stalled at the hope that this would be the moment he would finally put his foot down and make his intent with her known.

Kofi stared down at her, then back to Dante. He took his time, although Cindy was a fidgety mess.

"Nah, you got it," Kofi said as he threw her a wink and an upward nod to Dante.

"Kofi?"

"Yes." His hands were tucked inside his pockets as he awaited her response.

"Never mind."

Cindy allowed Dante to pull her to him, annoyed by his presence.

Chapter Four

Felicia's words from the night of the homecoming afterparty rattled in his mind. Maybe he'd failed yet another test. Was he supposed to tell Dante to step off when he tried to cut in like he wanted to? Is that what she responded to? Kofi didn't want to force himself on her. It was her choice who she wanted to dance with.

She may have been in Dante's arms, but her eyes and her body belonged to him. Cindy kept her gaze on him during their dance and throughout the night. He'd been turned on when she tussled with another woman for the bouquet. Her new sister, Stasia, pulled him to the middle for the garter toss. She was cute, but Kofi didn't buy into any of those wedding traditions, and she wasn't the Miller he wanted.

If Cindy hadn't taken notice, he would have remained in his seat. He stood inches taller than every other man near him. Only two seemed interested in catching it. One was in his thirties and likely ready to settle down, and the other clearly wanted to impress his date. Alonzo looked in Kofi's direction, turned his back, then threw it at him.

Mama Tremaine squealed in delight when she saw that he caught it.

"You know what that means," Alonzo's colleague who acted as the deejay announced. "Cindy Ella and the bald brotha who caught the garter, please make your way to the center. Everyone else, clear the dance floor."

Cindy sat in a chair and nervously shifted under Kofi's gaze. The song transitioned to a wordless instrumental, and all eyes fell on Kofi. He took the garter and spun it around his finger. Cindy was right where he wanted her. He could appreciate the rise and fall of her chest as she awaited his next move. He ambled in her direction, unbothered and unhurried.

He lowered to one knee once he was in front of her.

Confident that no one could hear what he said over the music and the hushed chatter, he said, "I can smell you."

Cindy's eyes drifted closed. When they opened, he saw lustful fire in them. He inched up the satin fabric of her thin gown, that looked like it was crafted for the bedroom, until it was above her knee.

"Alright now," Cindy's new stepmother hollered.

He removed one of her heels and gently placed it beside him.

"You alright?"

Cindy nodded.

"Want me to stop?"

She shook her head. "Please don't."

She was close to her dad, and she was obviously an adult, but there was no way he'd pull something like this in front of his parents. Cindy didn't seem to mind. He took the garter and placed it on her foot. It drove her wild when he moved leisurely, so he'd do it until he would damn near bring her to climax.

Kofi kept his eyes on Cindy and only moved them to stare at her full lips. The lipstick she wore made him harden. It was difficult not to think lewd thoughts when he studied her features. With one hand, he inched the garter belt up the smooth skin of her calf. A groan escaped his throat, and by the way she swallowed, she had no complaints.

Once it was above her knee, she let out a moan of her own. A lazy smile covered his face, and for the first time since they'd been in the center of the reception, he showcased his chip-toothed smile... the one that made her wet. His large hand covered her thigh beneath her dress where he positioned the garter. But he rested it there longer than necessary.

Cindy squeezed her eyes shut like maybe she was on the verge of an orgasm. He used his finger and traced tight circles on her warm skin. At that point, he didn't give a damn who watched. Another whimper escaped her sinful mouth, and she clamped her teeth around her bottom lip. He leaned his body toward her and kissed her gently, while those in attendance erupted in applause and whistles.

The deejay's announcement of the next item on the agenda for the night was background noise to Kofi. His attention was focused on Cindy. Her mind may have been at war about what she wanted, but her body belonged to him. It was clear now. He lifted and reached his hand down to pull her up.

She took it without hesitation. Kofi brought her body to him for a hug and whispered against her ear. "You could have that anytime you want."

Cindy released a breath, but she had yet to say anything. It was fine by him because he could read every desire and word her body communicated. He preferred it that way. He leaned in and kissed her on the cheek.

"Sorry to interrupt whatever this is," Dreeyah started, "but the photographer needs us for pictures."

She didn't hang around to wait for Cindy. Dreeyah delivered the message and sauntered off. Cindy's new sisters looked alike, but they couldn't be more different. Frankly, Kofi was convinced Stasia secretly had a thing for him.

"I gotta go."

"I heard. It's kind of late to ask this now, but was it OK that I came? Your dad invited me."

"I'm glad you came. I wish you wouldn't always ask for my permission."

"How else will I know what you're comfortable with?"

Her eyes lowered, and Kofi was positive his cousin was right. Although Cindy was a lady and she deserved to be treated like one, she wanted him to do as he pleased. Little did she know, that was a dangerous game where he was concerned. If it was up to him, he'd follow her body's lead and never utter a word. But he was taught to ask permission.

"They're waiting for me."

He hadn't released her yet, and now that she'd told him not to ask, he wasn't sure he wanted to let her go. He moved the hair that framed her face and pulled her chin up to him. He kissed her one last time. When he peered down at her, her eyes were still closed.

"Felicia and I are probably heading out soon, but I'm gonna call you."

"You do that." The sides of Cindy's sensual mouth lifted. She placed her hand on his head and added, "I like this, by the way. A lot."

* * *

Kofi was on cloud nine after the wedding. His work schedule was busy, and he just didn't have the nerve to tell Cindy what she would or wouldn't do. He also had no plans to share her with Dante. They texted over the next few months, but he hadn't been in her space since February. The April first date was fitting since he'd been a fool not to step up where Cindy was concerned.

She and Dante may have made things official. He'd been able to ignore Felicia's taunting and breeze past his brothers' antics who still hadn't gotten over their confrontation. They'd taken to giving him the silent treatment. He loved his brothers and wished they could get along, but he couldn't be solely responsible for the state of their relationships, no matter how much his mother said he was the mature one.

He'd arrived at work early Friday morning with more pep in his step. He still required coffee, but nothing could bring him down. Kofi had developed a rhythm in his time at Paradise Pet Care Hospital. Most of the staff had finally come to see him as more of an equal as opposed to his former role as an intern. It was a relief for Kofi not to be questioned at every turn.

"Interns are here."

Kofi looked up, and Johns had a creepy grin on his face. There went his good vibes. He checked the screen of his smart watch.

"Orientation is today?"

"Yep. And I wish it was their first day instead. Those girls are fine."

Kofi stood. He was both disgusted with Johns and hopeful for another chance to be close to Cindy. "I thought you worked with HR to keep your money up," Kofi teased. "The last thing you need is a harassment complaint."

Johns opened his mouth to respond, but Kofi left before he had the chance.

"This is our own Dr. Kofi," Ava purred.

Why were the interns with—. His thoughts were interrupted when he saw Cindy on her knees with a patient. Her back was to him, but he recognized her bright red hair and her impeccable ass. Those soft mounds rested comfortably on her heels as she fluffed the dog's ears. The patient's owner was in tears.

"He hadn't played with anyone in weeks. Whatever slowed him down doesn't seem to matter with you, Dr.?"

"Cindy. You can call me Cindy." She stood, and Kofi worried he wouldn't be able to calm his accelerated libido. He had his work cut out to remain professional in his new position with her as an intern if he struggled this badly with the sight of her in her blush-colored scrubs.

"How long have his eyes been red?"

Kofi blinked himself awake. He'd been so enamored with Cindy's body that he hadn't noticed she'd started with the patient's history. She wasn't here to practice; she was here to orient herself to the practice. Some of the other interns whispered about how she was a know-it-all.

He cleared his throat and stepped forward. "I'm Kofi Carter. Cindy is one of our promising interns."

He watched her cheeks tint, and he didn't miss her using her tongue to wet her lips.

"Can she be in the room for Tiny's exam?"

"Tiny?" Kofi and Cindy asked in unison.

The Cane Corso was probably a little under one hundred pounds.

"He hasn't responded to anyone since he fell ill. He likes her," the woman insisted.

Cindy's eyes were large and expressive. She was hopeful, but all Kofi wanted was to take her in the nearest vacant room and finish what they started at homecoming.

"She sure can," Johns declared.

Kofi looked down to see the balding man motion for Cindy to follow them into a patient room. His breaths were shallow. He wanted to forbid it, but the words wouldn't come out. *Fuck!*

Ava had taken over while the intern coordinator attended to a phone call. She kept her eyes on him the entire time. Out of the small group of seven, three were young men. He introduced himself to the group and did his best not to check the exam room where Cindy was every two seconds.

"Most of what you hear today, you're likely going to forget."

A few of them laughed, but one of the guys had a notepad and took notes feverishly.

"Except him." Kofi pointed at the intern who reminded him of himself. "When is your official start date?"

"Me?"

Kofi nodded.

"August twenty-second."

"Cool. I was an intern before I got hired. Wanna see where you're going to spend most of your time?"

It wouldn't take much to convince them. They were about to clear the hall when the patient door flew open. The owner's smile was wide and matched the one Cindy wore. Johns, however, was red in the face and muttered incoherently as he bumped into Kofi.

"Everything okay?"

"It's like having you as a baby doctor all over again."

Kofi chuckled, but Johns was fiercely serious. He pushed his way past the interns and huffed when Kofi introduced him to the other students.

"Don't mind Dr. Johns. He's always like that."

* * *

It was one thing to see Kofi at the wedding, but now that time had passed, the sight of him in a position of power had Cindy's mind twisted. His laid-back demeanor was one of his most attractive qualities. Somehow, she expected him to be uptight since this was his first position as a veterinarian. He wasn't. Kofi was like a fish in water.

The legal paperwork for an intern was soul-crushing. The other interns weren't open to easy conversation with her, which wasn't a surprise. Most of Cindy's friends had four legs. The cafeteria was like a scene straight from her high school.

The other interns all sat engulfed in a private discussion. There was barely space at the table they occupied. Some of the doctors seemed friendly, but she didn't want to give any of them the wrong impression about who she was and what she had to offer. Then there was Kofi. She hoped she wouldn't get him into any trouble.

"Can I sit here?"

He lifted his eyes from her waist to her face and smirked. He nodded.

"Thanks. I thought I was gonna have to go and find Tiny."

"Or Dante," he muttered.

Cindy looked down at her meal. Dante was a nonfactor. If he asked, she'd tell him.

"What's up with him? That your man?"

Cindy shook her head.

"Good."

He dropped it, and she was both frustrated and relieved. This would be her job until she officially got hired as a doctor or found permanent employment elsewhere. She preferred if that was her focus.

"How did it go with Johns?"

She cringed. "About that..."

Kofi released a deep belly laugh. "What'd you do, girl?"

"I may have told her that Tiny was fat."

Kofi's face straightened, and he searched hers for any hint of laughter. "You did what?"

"I said there was nothing wrong with her dog other than the fact that he's fat. Tiny's not that different from her. If she sat home for hours and ate without moving, would she have the energy to engage cheerfully with others?"

Kofi's mouth hung open.

"What?" Cindy shrugged. It was the truth. *Does anyone respect honesty these days?*

Kofi grasped her hand across the table and intertwined his fingers with hers. "I think I love you."

She snatched away then leaned over the table to swat his chest. "Be serious."

"Did you actually say all that?"

"Where's the lie, Dr. Carter?"

With his eyes still on hers, he pulled his phone from his scrubs. He typed a message then returned his gaze to hers.

Dr. Kofi Carter: you remember what happened last time you looked at me

Her phone chimed. When she pulled it out and read his text, it made her squirm in her seat.

Cindy: I wasn't looking at you

Dr. Kofi Carter: you may as well with the way you just said Dr. Carter. Shit is as dangerous as the way you looked at me during your father's wedding.

Dr. Kofi Carter: I don't have the garter, but I still have my hand and my tongue

Cindy sucked in a breath and peered around the cafeteria. She felt his leg bump against hers under the table. Her flesh heated beneath the fabric of her scrubs from their brief contact.

"How's your new family?" he asked as if he hadn't texted her with panty dropping rhetoric that made her reconsider her decision about Kofi Carter.

"They're great. I've always wanted a sibling. Now I have two," she sang.

"That makes one of us."

"Why do you say that?"

"Your sisters are different," he announced. He swerved her inquiry about his statement, but she didn't mind. She'd rather talk about her new family than be hot and bothered by his flirty texts.

"You just have to warm up to them."

"They're like night and day. One of them looked like she wanted to clock me in the jaw—"

"Dreeyah. She's mostly harmless."

"Yeah, okay. And the other one... she seemed interested."

"Stasia. We share taste in men."

Kofi's chipped-tooth smile beamed in her direction. "Mrs. Miller too, huh?"

Cindy nodded. "She definitely likes you."

The timer on Kofi's cell phone rang. "Break time is over. Someone else is going to finish the day with you and the other interns."

Cindy's smile faded. She didn't know what the hell she wanted with Kofi Carter, especially when he couldn't consistently assert himself with her, but she appreciated being in his presence here more than anything.

"When I call you later, pick up," he said as he stood.

It's about damn time! "Okay."

* * *

Orientation came to an end, and Cindy still didn't have her daily dose of animal love. Gus tolerated her, but today, she wanted more. On the way home, she stopped at a local shelter and walked a few dogs to help the severely overworked staff. With her cup full, she navigated to her new home and family.

"Cindy, what is that smell?"

She'd barely closed the door and removed her shoes when Dreeyah met her with her fingers pinched at the bridge of her nose. Cindy would shower straight away, but her sisters and Mama Tremaine weren't big animal people.

"I stopped by the animal rescue after orientation."

"Why? You know what, don't answer that."

Cindy opened her arms as if she would hug Dreeyah. She giggled and used her body to block her sister's path.

"You smell like wet dog," Dreeyah said as she ducked to miss Cindy's embrace.

"Love you too, sis."

Dreeyah sucked her teeth and quickly left the room. Cindy whirled around her home and hummed, "A dream is a wish your heart makes." As she ascended the stairs, Gus was on his way down. She leaned in his direction and allowed him to jump on her shoulder. His yellow, feline eyes put Cindy at ease. Gus was a home within a home.

"Is that you, Cindy Ella?" Stasia called out from upstairs.

"It is," she sang as she rubbed Gus. "I missed you today," she said to her favorite feline.

"How was orientation?" Stasia asked when Cindy was a few feet away.

Gus's tail went horizontal, and he hissed. He'd been standoffish with Cindy and Alonzo's new family members, but she had never seen him behave this way. Burmese cats loved people and strangers. Cindy set him down and watched him scurry out of sight. *That's strange.*

"Hey, sis," Cindy said. She leaned in, and unlike Dreeyah, Stasia gave her a warm hug, despite her work scrubs. "Sorry I smell like animal."

"You're a vet, silly. Of course, you do."

"It went well. I hate that it's so far from our official start date. It was a tease. Animals are my love language, and they want me to do what exactly until August?" Cindy's voice was light and airy, although she worried if she had the patience to make it through the summer.

"Did you see the good doctor?" Stasia asked.

Cindy didn't have the heart to tell her new sister that she and Kofi had history. They weren't official, but the more Kofi took charge with and around her, the more Cindy responded. The corners of her lips lifted of their own accord, and her hips swayed. "I did."

She whirled toward her bathroom and sang, "When you're fast asleep." When Cindy got to the door, her eyes landed on her bonus sister who hadn't moved. Stasia's expression was unrecognizable, but when she saw Cindy's gaze focused on her, she forced a smile. Cindy didn't expect to be as close with the twins as they were with each other. But just like Gus, the girls would grow to accept her cheery disposition. She meant no harm.

Cindy was still amazed at how wonderful her new shower felt. Her charged body wash and bath oils were amplified by the waterfall style shower head. The additional three body sprays were like a luxury car wash for humans. There was nothing like a shower to ground her. Except for a dozen princess parties, Cindy's life would slow for the first time since she completed vet school.

She dressed in yoga pants and an off the shoulder shirt with woodland creatures on it. She purposefully picked her comfy clothes since it was Friday. And Friday was movie night. She and her dad had tried for the last month to get Mama Tremaine and her sisters to participate in their weekly tradition, but each week, someone was unable to make it.

Alonzo was an easy-going man. He didn't ask for much and was quite accommodating, so when he insisted everyone be available for this week's movie night, the family agreed. The four of them gathered in the loft area with the largest TV.

"The top-rated movies are, *A Soul's Unrest: The Haunting of Damon Daniels* or *The Accidental Engagement*," Alonzo said. He scratched his brow and observed the four loves of his life.

"This is an easy one!" Cindy squealed.

"Let's vote. Raise your hand if you want to watch *The Accidental Engagement*," Alonzo instructed.

Cindy's hand flew up, but as she peered at the other women, her arm sagged.

Dreeyah snickered. "Come on. You can't be serious. How is an accidental engagement even possible?"

"That's why we watch, to figure out how it happens," she responded to Dreeyah. "Stasia?" Cindy asked. She and Dreeyah had completely different tastes, but she and Stasia had lots in common.

Stasia shrugged. "The first one got better reviews. I've been waiting to see it."

Cindy was content to watch the movie as a family. She didn't fancy thriller or horror films, but she was up for an opportunity to bond. "Hey. Does anybody call you Anastasia?"

An eerie hush settled across the room. Alonzo and Cindy wore matching confused expressions on their faces. Mama Tremaine rested her hand across her chest, and Dreeyah shook her head.

"What? What did I say?" Cindy asked, full of hesitation. Whatever she'd done was a mistake. She wanted to ensure she didn't make it again.

"My dad called me that," Stasia muttered with a ghosted look on her face.

"Oh. My mom wanted me to be called Cynthia."

"It's not the same," Stasia snapped. "My dad wasn't some perfect parent gone too soon. He was a bad man. And I hate that name. There's a reason I go by Stasia."

Cindy was caught off guard by her tone. She wouldn't have been surprised if it was Dreeyah who set her straight, but this was strange coming from Stasia. Her father must have been awful.

"I'm sorry."

"You couldn't have known," Mama Tremaine said as she laid a hand on Stasia's leg.

Cindy wanted to crawl out of her skin and scurry away like Gus had earlier.

"You okay?" Alonzo asked as he took a seat between Cindy and Stasia.

She nodded and gave him a weak smile.

"It's all good, sis," Stasia said to Cindy with sincerity.

What a relief!

"Three votes for *A Soul's Unrest: The Haunting of Damon Daniels.*"

"I'll grab snacks. Anyone want popcorn?" Cindy asked. She needed to move her body to shake the awkward moment where she stuck her foot in her mouth.

"Sounds good, Ella," Alonzo added.

Luckily, the movie hadn't been gory. The woman was shot and killed in the opening credits. She was survived by her two daughters, son, and her husband. They were wealthy, and there was speculation she'd been murdered over money.

"I bet it's the husband. They always suspect the spouse," Stasia mumbled.

"It's the neighbor. That lady is hella nosy," Dreeyah added.

"Aye," Alonzo said as he threw a cushion in her direction. "Language."

It was rare for Dreeyah to smile, but Alonzo had a good track record with putting her in a good mood. It warmed Cindy's heart to see how close they were. She adored her father. He had enough love to go around.

"I don't trust her mother with her beady eyes," Mama Tremaine offered.

"Hmm," Cindy said.

"What do you think, Cindy Ella?" Mama Tremaine probed.

"I don't wanna ruin the movie," she insisted.

"You assume you know for a fact," Stasia said and kissed her teeth. "I thought you didn't like thrillers."

Cindy considered her words. Stasia was no longer a fan of hers. What changed? Was it the way she used her full name? Or was this about Kofi? *Shit.*

"It's one of the reasons I don't like thrillers. They're easy to guess." Cindy shrugged and tried to refocus on the movie. She hoped they'd let it go.

Dreeyah swiped the remote and paused it. "Now you have to share this theory. If I didn't think Alonzo would put me in time out, I'd bet money on it," Dreeyah teased.

"Correct. No gambling," he said as he nodded.

Cindy tucked her legs beneath her. "It's the son."

All heads craned in her direction. She wished they could have watched the romantic comedy—those movies and animals were her happy place.

"Everyone else genuinely looks sad or at least confused as to why the woman was murdered. Every time they show him, he's fidgety. Maybe he did it by accident," Cindy guessed.

"Let's finish and see," Alonzo said.

He was predictable. Alonzo would be asleep in less than an hour. He wanted to finish the movie before his battery died.

The credits rolled, and her bonus sisters' eyes were on her. The son and father were both named Damon, but it was the son who was haunted until he told the truth about how he killed his mom and tried to cover it up. Cindy scolded herself for opening her big mouth. She should have lied.

Dreeyah and Stasia said goodnight to Alonzo and their mother and gave her a forced wave. Cindy stood, and Mama Tremaine followed her.

"Cindy Ella," she called out.

Cindy fiddled with her hair. All she wanted since she was a child was a mother. Now that she had Mama Tremaine, the last thing she wanted was to upset her because she couldn't get along with the twins.

"Give them time," she cooed.

Cindy nodded. A knot formed in her throat. She would do anything for a hug at that moment, but she was awkward about how to ask. As if Mama Tremaine could sense it, she pulled Cindy into the space between her collarbone and chin and hugged her tightly. Cindy melted into her. They stood wordlessly for long moments.

Finally, Cindy found her voice. "Thank you."

Mama Tremaine lifted her chin. "You know what you need?"

Cindy shook her head.

"You need some alone time with your dad."

She wasn't sure why, but tears filled Cindy's eyes. She wanted time with her new family, but it hadn't dawned on her until Mama Tremaine's suggestion, that she deeply missed one-on-one moments with her father. *How did she do that?*

"Mothers know." Mama Tremaine grasped Cindy's cheeks between her hands and planted a reassuring kiss on her forehead. "Let me know if you need us to clear out, or if you want to plan the date yourself."

They hugged one last time, and once again, Cindy's hopeful spirit was renewed.

Chapter Five

It was May, and Cindy had a princess gig scheduled. Something about this job was off, but she couldn't put her finger on what it was. Her intuition spoke to her through feelings that couldn't be explained with words. The decorations were right, but everything else was... wrong.

What would drive a parent to host a princess party for a child in the late evening on Friday the thirteenth was beyond her. While she didn't buy into the notion that the day held spooky powers, she was aware that many did.

"Hi, Cindy."

Cindy whipped around to see a small girl in an all-white gown. She was stunning, but her eyes held a wisdom that didn't match her five short years. Cindy knelt in front of her. Her gown encased her so that her legs were entirely hidden beneath. It added a magical touch to her royal persona for the children.

"How did you know my name?" She'd only offered her princess name, Ginger, to the group.

"My name Oya, but my parents named me Leena. I know stuff. That's why they don't play with me much."

The little girl pointed toward the other children who twirled in their dresses and giggled uncontrollably. Of course, they didn't want to play with her. She'd announced herself as Oya, then followed it up with the name her parents gave her. Her soul was ancient, but the conversation was disturbing.

"I'm sure I could find a game for us all to play. What else do you know?"

Cindy was notoriously left out during play when she was younger, because the kids bullied her for not having a mom. It hurt her deeply, and as an adult, she made it her mission to ensure she engaged with the seemingly unpopular children.

"I know about Alonzo. He leavin' soon. He's gonna be with my gram before the Blood Moon." Leena's eyes hadn't wavered. She was locked in on Cindy like she could read her entire lineage.

"How did you know... Where is your gram?" Cindy whirled around to see if the child's grandmother was at the party.

The fact that this strange child said Alonzo's name made the hairs on the back of Cindy's neck stand. Nothing that included her father and an insinuation of death was to be taken lightly.

"My gram is on the other side... with Ms. Celina. They all together without they bodies."

Cindy gasped and slapped her hand against her mouth. She had never seen the little girl before tonight. Celina Miller was her mother's name. There was no way Leena could have guessed information that personal. Cindy's hands trembled in front of her face.

"What does my dad... Alonzo have to do with your gram and my mom... my... Celina?" Cindy's eyes blinked rapidly as she tried to determine if the conversation was a mean prank.

"Alonzo is getting out of his body soon. You should say bye like I said bye to Gram. She was happy when I told her she was goin' 'cause her body had hurts on it everywhere."

"Who told you my mom and dad's names?" Cindy demanded.

"You don't hear good. I said I know stuff."

"Everything OK, Ginger?" The birthday girl's mother, Tolanda, gave Cindy a bright smile and Leena a chilly once over. Her presence was unwelcomed by children and adults alike.

It was a conscious decision to use a stage name when she did the princess parties. Cindy went by the name Ginger. The fact that the little girl addressed her by her first name was unnerving.

Leena skipped away and joined the other children. She waved in slow motion as Cindy and the woman looked on.

"The things she said to me. Nobody could have guessed the names she used."

"We've had a few run-ins with little Miss Leena. She did some kind of creepy wish and killed our dog." Talonda folded and refolded a hand towel at the kitchen island as she spoke.

With furrowed brows, Cindy asked, "She did what?"

Talonda filled Cindy in on the tragedy of their barely three-year-old dog who passed away suddenly. Apparently, there was a clot in his lungs. He was fine until he wasn't. Leena told Talonda's daughter that her dog was going to go to sleep and never wake up again. Talonda was positive there was a connection between what Leena told her and what happened to their family pet.

As the party came to an end, Cindy stepped outside to call her father. She needed to hear his voice.

"Ella, I was just thinking about you," Alonzo said into his phone.

"Daddy."

"Yes, Ella."

She held the phone, unsure of why the knot in her stomach hadn't eased. Her friends from college taunted her about how odd young kids were and questioned how she could find enjoyment in entertaining them in the way she did. Today was the first time she understood the sentiment.

"Cynthia, honey, you're scaring me."

She could hear her father excuse himself. The background noise was now nonexistent.

"Are you okay, Daddy?" She barely recognized her voice. Maybe he was sick and hadn't shared it with her. She couldn't wrap her head around why she was in the emotional state she was. Yet, the idea that her father would join Leena's possibly dead gram sent shockwaves of fear through her system.

"Yes. Are you okay, love?"

Tears streamed down her cheeks as she watched families gather their party favors and children.

"Do you think Mom would have taken me to princess parties like the ones I do?"

Alonzo exhaled a heavy breath. "Your mom would have loved nothing more."

Cindy wiped her tears and gave a picture-perfect smile to the guests as they filed out. Talonda could pay her electronically. Generally, Cindy would wait until the party was over and offer to entertain any remaining guests and the birthday girl while the parents cleaned. There was no way she could be of service in that capacity tonight.

She shuffled to her car as her father continued.

"You wanna talk about it, Ella?"

She shook her head. She didn't have the heart to put words to Leena's bizarre warning. Even now she could recall the sincerity in the child's voice.

"Ella?"

"It's going to sound insane. No, I don't want to talk about it. How are things going with you and Mama Tremaine?"

Through what sounded like his wide signature smile, Alonzo responded, "Things are going well. Did I ever tell you about the time I took your mom to one of those character theme parks?"

"Yes, but tell me again."

A calm washed over Cindy as she pushed the events of the day from her mind. Although she had a new mom and two bonus sisters, her dad was the closest person she had in the world. He understood and accepted her. And she'd be damned if she let her mind get the best of her.

* * *

Dr. Kofi Carter: You busy?

Cindy: It depends

Dr. Kofi Carter: I'm going on site for the job today, and I could use an extra set of hands

Cindy: When? Where?

Dr. Kofi Carter: Is that a yes?

Cindy: Of course

Dr. Kofi Carter: I hope I don't have to tell you to wear scrubs and your internship name tag. I'll be at your place around noon

Cindy squealed with excitement. She should have to wait until August to practice like the rest of her peers, but she had the hookup. Dr. Kofi Carter had requested her presence to help him with a job. It was his energy when he was in doctor mode that Cindy responded to. He was a gentleman when it came to her, which she could respect, but that behavior didn't make her kitty purr.

She had enough time to eat an early lunch and change out of her lounge clothes. Her mind reeled at what type of job it could be. What if they delivered a calf?

"Where are you headed, Ella? I thought your internship didn't start until the fall?" her father asked, confused. He was in his chair with coffee and a newspaper. The fact that they still printed them tickled her. "Don't tell me you're going back to the shelter? You never come home empty-handed."

Cindy rounded the corner and leaned down to hug him. "I love you, Daddy."

The corners of his mouth lifted. "I know what you're doing. I'm trying to keep a happy wife, and Tremaine doesn't like animals like we do," he pressed.

Through a spirited giggle, Cindy said, "I'm not going to the shelter, and I'm not bringing more animals home... today." She slipped out of his embrace.

"Ella."

"I'm kidding. Just Gus for now."

He frowned.

"Kofi's taking me on site."

"Ahhh, I see."

"It's not like that," she explained.

"Whatever you say." Alonzo picked his paper back up and stared at it with a smug smile on his face. "I saw the two of you at the wedding."

"Daddy!"

"You're an adult. And I've always liked Kofi. Looks like you like him too."

Cindy exhaled a frustrated breath. "This outing is about veterinary medicine."

"Oh, yes, the site. What does that mean exactly?"

"I don't know. I'm hoping we get to deliver a calf," Cindy exclaimed, her excitement at the surface once again.

"Your daughter is weird," Dreeyah announced as she shuffled through the living room, this time with her face in a book instead of her phone. She stumbled when Alonzo stretched his foot out in her direction. "One day, I'm going to break my neck, and you'll be sorry," she teased.

"I'd pay money to see you in a neck brace," Alonzo taunted.

"You heard that, Cindy. You're strange, and your dad is violent," she said with a smile. "And your chariot awaits."

Cindy looked in the direction of Dreeyah's bony finger—her countenance once again bored.

"Kofi."

"Have fun," her father sang.

She grabbed her water bottle and ran outside before Kofi could get out of his car.

"Hey," he said as she slammed the door and clicked her seat belt.

"Hey. Don't want to be late, right?"

Kofi hesitated but backed his car out of her driveway.

"Your family is going to think I'm rude," Kofi started.

"They won't. Trust me." Eager to change the subject, Cindy asked about their destination. "Where are we going?"

"I was the only one available to do a site visit today, and I needed an extra set of hands. And since I know one of the interns personally, here we are."

She blushed. The way he said he knew her made her palms perspire. "You told me that already. What's the job?"

"I'll let it be a surprise."

They continued the ten-minute drive to the outskirts of town in a comfortable silence. When they arrived at the farm, Cindy hopped out excited to deliver a baby. What a wonderful surprise. As they neared two farmers and their bull, it was clear she wouldn't see a birth on this visit.

"Kofi, is this a castration?" Cindy asked through gritted teeth.

He smirked at her but didn't respond.

"Dr. Carter, thank you for taking the time to come out. Our little guy is quite aggressive, and we need to get this over with."

"It won't be a problem. One of the best parts of the job," he lied.

"I couldn't do it," the man divulged as if it hurt him to consider.

"That's why we're here. This is my intern, Cindy. She's going to be my assistant, so if you want, you don't even have to watch!"

The two men smiled, and one released a loud sigh of relief. "Thank God."

"His name is Buck," the younger man said. "We'll leave you to it."

The men headed in the opposite direction as Kofi turned on his heels to get his equipment. Cindy stomped behind him, upset he didn't reveal the job before they got there.

"You'll have an edge over the other interns because you'll have assisted."

She rolled her eyes.

"I saw that," he teased.

He laid out the supplies near the bull and gave Cindy a quick safety briefing. "Just help me keep him calm."

The bull kicked incessantly.

"Should I go get one of them? What if he kicks us?"

"He won't." Kofi's voice wasn't crass, but it was direct and snapped Cindy out of her justified fear. "Distract him for thirty seconds, and I can at least start. The process takes about two minutes."

"Okay."

He stepped to the side of the wild bull whose neck was wedged between a head gate so he couldn't run away or see behind him. Kofi dawned thick gloves and instructed Cindy to hold the steer's tail while he grabbed the instrument with the band. Despite Cindy's prompt obedience, the bull continued to jerk and kick. The poor bull calf couldn't know Kofi and his practice chose the painless, bloodless method to apply a tight band to the testicles. Within a month, they would fall off on their own.

Nevertheless, she'd never forgive herself if Kofi got kicked in the process. She used her free hand to rub the steer's back and sang. "A dream is a wish your hmm hmm," she belted. The bull stopped. Besides her humming, clicks from Kofi tightening the band was the only sound on the clear summer afternoon. He walked around and released the bull's head. He finished in minutes, just as he promised.

"Thank you, Cindy," he said as he removed his gloves. Kofi beamed.

The bull finally backed away from her. Cindy was in awe. She loved this job.

* * *

She was beside herself on the drive back to her home. Cindy chatted Kofi's ear off about what they experienced with the bull and how she got her internship at Paradise Pet Care in the first place.

"She's like my fairy godmother." Cindy gushed.

Kofi swung his head in her direction. "You're a real-life princess, huh?"

She swatted him playfully. "Professor Brenton was more than a mentor to me while I was a student at Gullah. She was like a mother."

"You miss yours?" Kofi asked.

She nodded. "I never met her, but I'll always miss the space she should have occupied. On top of that, I'm an only child. No older siblings to share memories with."

"You're not missing out." Kofi's voice was strained when he spoke.

She shifted in her seat and faced him. "What's the deal with you and your brothers?"

"How you know I got brothers?"

"I overheard Felicia mention it."

He was quiet for a beat. "I have a strained relationship with my older brothers because I had to grow up quicker than they did."

"Why?"

He stole a glance in her direction. Under any other circumstance, he would have shut the conversation down, but her innocence and concern melted his resolve.

"I saw some fucked-up shit at a sleepover when I was young. It messes with me to this day because I didn't do the right thing."

"What happened?"

He was five minutes from Cindy's home, but she wouldn't let him drop it.

"It was my first night away from home and without my brothers. I couldn't stand the fact that my brother Devin snored, but once I didn't hear it, I couldn't sleep." Kofi chuckled at the memory.

"I heard a noise outside the upstairs window of my best friend, Jason's, house where the sleepover was. When I went to investigate what caused it, there was a woman being attacked."

Cindy gasped. She rested her hand over her heart as she listened.

"I'd seen that kind of shit in movies, but never in real life. She screamed, and she fought to get out of his grip. But it was so late, no one else was on the street to help her. He had on a black ski mask and gloves, and he wouldn't let her go. He opened the door and struggled to get her inside.

"I had two choices: I could go and get an adult, or I could watch and try to see the license plate number for the car, or anything else that would help the police find her."

"What did you do?" Cindy asked. Her voice was shaky.

"I went and woke up an adult. Before I could find someone to come to the window, the man had gotten the woman in his car and took off."

"Kofi," Cindy rasped.

"Jason's parents called the police, but they asked identifying questions I didn't have the answers to. I had more information about the woman than I did the aggressor which wouldn't help anything. If she reported the assault, which I know you're aware most don't, nothing I saw would bring her any justice."

Cindy rested her hand on his thigh. "Did you tell your brothers, and they didn't believe you or something?"

"I never told anyone after that night. Didn't mention it to my parents or siblings. But I was never the same after that. Suddenly, I was a laid-back child who observed more than I spoke. The girls at school called me shit like mysterious. All the while, I let that woman down. If only I hadn't been so slow to move or if I had gotten the plate number."

"You can't do that to yourself. How old were you?" she probed.

"Twelve."

"There's no way you could have known the exact right response. I'd guess most adults wouldn't have handled it much differently."

"What if that was my mom or Felicia? I wouldn't give a damn if the person who saw was scared," he swore.

He parked at the curb of Cindy's castle-like home. It fit her in every way.

She shifted her body in the passenger seat to face him. "You weren't just scared. You were a child. You gotta let yourself off the hook for this."

He huffed and gazed out of the window. She was right, but he had no clue how to go about that process. He felt her soft hand on his face as she turned it to look at him.

"I'm sorry you had to go through that."

"Don't be. People have gone through worse."

"True. But that doesn't negate your experience, Kofi."

They were quiet for long moments, as he tried to process her words.

"Can I ask you a question?" She continued.

He nodded. At this point, why not?

"What was Kofi like before all of this?"

He smiled, and in return, she did too.

He turned his body toward her. "Honestly?"

"Yep."

"I was a little like you."

Her mouth fell open. "You were a wild and free Prince Kofi?"

He hummed his response and undid his seat belt to lean closer to her.

"You want to know a secret?" he asked as he invaded her space.

"Yes," she said on an exhale.

"I'm still a prince." He saw her eyes widen right before he kissed her deeply.

Kofi wanted Cindy before, but now that she'd allowed him to be completely vulnerable without judgment, he made it his mission to clear any doubt from her mind that they belonged together.

Chapter Six

Kofi paced the creaky floor of his cramped room. He'd let another two weeks slip by without taking Cindy out like he said he would when he saw her at orientation. Although she'd accompanied him for the job, they had yet to go on a date. Today, he was fortunate enough to have Friday off work. His shifts were long, and between his tense home situation and the help he offered his parents, he didn't have the energy for much else.

"You need to get out of here," Felicia said as she plopped down on Kofi's bed.

He and his cousin were closer than he was with his own siblings. She was notorious for visits at the ass crack of dawn. Felicia told her dates she lived at her cousin's address when she first met them. If they had the balls to pop up, they would be met with the unhinged Carter men. They only had to greet one of her guys. After their little chat, he never called Felicia again.

"I told my dad I'd stay for another year to help out."

"That too, but I meant today. It's Friday, and I know you miss the princess."

"Cindy."

"Exactly," she said as she scrolled through her phone.

"And who's the lucky old balls who dropped you off?"

She stood and smoothed her clothes as she looked in the floor-length mirror. She fluffed her 'fro and applied lip gloss.

"Nigel."

Kofi guffawed. "Where did you meet him?"

Felicia scowled at him. "At least I'm going out. You got all these jokes, but did you and princess Cindy ever finish what you started all those months ago?"

Kofi had Cindy right where he wanted her at the wedding, then again at orientation with his promise to call her later, and their time with the bull calf had been extra special. But once again, he let too much time slip by. Kofi was beyond frustrated with their misaligned schedules. And when it came to dating, Cindy only responded to him when he told her and not when he asked. A part of him was afraid he'd enjoy it too much—maybe take things too far when it came to decisions on his terms. It was a new power he was only accustomed to during sex.

He gazed down at his phone faced up on the bed Felicia had just abandoned. *Fuck it.*

Kofi: Be ready in an hour. I'm taking you out

Cindy: It's early

Kofi: I know

Cindy: It's too early for company. Everyone is in the house. My dad isn't even awake yet

Kofi: Your people like me

Cindy: That's the problem. You'd never leave

Kofi: Get dressed in comfortable clothes. Jeans and long sleeves

Cindy: make me

Kofi: Don't tempt me. I'll knock on the front door with flowers in my hand

*Cindy: Fine! Text me when you get here. Park a few houses down like I'm back in high school. I'm definitely hiding you *eye roll emoji*

Kofi: It'll be worth it.

Kofi: You might not wanna see me, but I know your pussy does

She didn't write back. He could only imagine her face when she read his last text. It was much easier for him to assert himself over the phone.

"Finally made plans with her?"

"Yup, now get out."

Felicia accepted a call as Kofi pushed her toward the door. "Save all that for your princess," she sassed. "My cousin Kofi," Felicia said into her phone. "I'm on my way to work," she lied.

As Kofi slammed the door to prepare for his morning date, Felicia yelled, "Bye, Aunt Norma and Uncle Sammie!" The clacking sound of her footsteps returned to his door. "Bye, big head."

Kofi texted a friend from vet school who owed him a favor. If Cindy was as whimsical as she seemed, sunrise would be the perfect date. The early morning spring climate was breezy—at this early hour, it was hoodie or light jacket weather. He dressed in record time and packed an extra hoodie in case Cindy got cold.

Kofi said good morning to his mother and ignored Maurice who sucked his teeth as Kofi headed out. He stopped at the store to pick up a few items they might need, then navigated to Cindy's home. When he arrived, he had half a mind to knock on her front door no matter what she said. He was raised to look a woman's father in the eye before he took her out.

Alonzo wouldn't let him drop by though. In that sense, Cindy was right. He'd want to invite him in and catch up, and Kofi wasn't in the head space to be near her interested twin sister. The cobalt blue sky announced the blue hour—thirty minutes before sunrise. He texted her so they would make it to their destination as he planned.

Kofi: Come outside

Cindy: Make me

Kofi: If I get out this car, I won't be the one who regrets it

*Cindy: I'm cumming *tongue out laughing emoji*

Kofi: Keep playing

Movement in his rearview mirror caught his attention. He saw her stallion-like figure, and his pants tightened. She was stealthy, and her long legs gave the appearance that she danced more than walked. Kofi craned his neck behind him. He couldn't keep his cool—he tracked her frame until she stood before his car.

He hopped out and shuffled to her side. She feigned annoyance, but he saw the slight smirk across her full lips.

"Where are you taking me?"

He reached beside her as if he'd grab her, but simply opened the door for her to get in. She didn't need to know until they arrived. Cindy's smirk deepened as she sat then swung both of her legs in.

"Damn," Kofi said.

In sneakers, fitted jeans, and a white long-sleeve thermal, she was breathtaking. She moved like she wore an expensive gown, and it turned him on. He'd never seen a woman get into a car the way she did.

Kofi folded into his vehicle and navigated to the southern coast. The ride took them less than fifteen minutes. He bounced his eyes between the road and the hypnotic woman in his passenger side. They didn't speak, but her melodic hums tickled his ears. His date would score him major points, although he would have been satisfied to simply enjoy a quiet ride with her.

When he parked and Cindy saw the three beautiful horses, her eyes lit up, and she jumped out of the car before he had a chance to open her door.

"What did you do?" she asked as she jiggled and squealed in delight.

Kofi threw a wink her way. He grabbed her hand and intertwined their fingers as they headed toward Kofi's friend.

"Hey, Brian," Kofi said.

"Dr. Carter," Brian responded with a sly smile. "Who is this beautiful lady? And what's she doing with you?"

"This is my date, Cynthia Miller," Kofi said.

Cindy accepted his hand with a blush. "Just Cindy."

Brian gave a safety briefing then allowed them a few moments with their horses.

"If you're both comfortable, we can get going. I have strict orders to start your ride during sunrise and the golden hour."

Kofi sucked his teeth.

"In school, he was always going on about the proper names for the time of day. The blue hour, sunset, the golden hour etcetera," he teased.

Kofi was about to respond with a snarky remark but was interrupted with the sensual way Cindy mounted her horse. His mouth went dry. What had he done?

The ride was peaceful. The sounds of nature paired with the clapping of the horses' feet put him in a meditative state. Every now and then, his eyes would fixate on the movement of Cindy's hips as she rode ahead of him. She turned around and caught him with his eyes on her ass. He gave her his chipped-tooth smile and threw her a quick wink.

"You ready?" Brian called behind him.

"Yes, sir," Kofi responded.

He led the horses toward the water and stopped at the water's edge. Kofi guided his horse beside Cindy's.

"We're going in the water."

Her eyes were wide, but he refused to ask if she was okay with it.

Brian entered with his horse, and Kofi motioned for Cindy to follow. They started their walk in shallow water, and when they were confident the horses were comfortable, they continued until their legs were submerged beneath the water. Brian was ahead, with Cindy and Kofi side by side. She beamed in his direction.

"Told you it would be worth it."

Cindy grabbed his hand and leaned her body toward him. He'd never forgive himself if she fell from her horse or hurt herself in any way, so he quickly planted a kiss on her lips.

"It's the most romantic date I've ever been on. A horseback ride and swim at sunrise? You've outdone yourself."

✳ ✳ ✳

Kofi had a fresh pair of clothes for them once the date was over. They changed in the bathroom of his friend Brian's guest ranch. The clothes Kofi brought for her were snug. They showcased her curves in a way that would please him more than her. Had he done that intentionally? Cindy smiled to herself as she swirled in the bathroom mirror. Kofi was more of a gentleman than she preferred, but he'd shown he could take charge.

She stepped out and smiled when her eyes connected with his chipped-tooth smile.

"Damn, you look good. You hungry?" he asked as he peered down at her.

Before she could answer, a yawn escaped her lips. A day with Kofi would be great, but unless he would let her nap, she wouldn't enjoy it.

"I am."

"I feel like a thick round but is about to come next."

She giggled. "I'm sleepy. Take me home, please."

He was disappointed. Cindy didn't doubt she could make it up to him later. She leaned her body against his and stuffed her hands in the pocket of his hoodie. Despite the layers of fabric between them, she felt him stiffen. She pressed her lips against his and melted into him when he deepened the kiss. Their tongues tangled. They only stopped when Brian cleared his throat.

"Get a room," he said after he'd locked up.

"You opened just for us?" she asked, still close to Kofi.

"I owed him. We're even now, Carter."

They waved goodbye and watched as his truck backed out onto the country road.

"Let me take you out again tonight," Kofi proposed when Brian's car disappeared.

Kofi's scent wafted into her nose. The masculine remnants of sweat and deodorant threatened to wake her from her sluggish state. He draped his arm around her shoulder and awaited her response.

"After I sleep, I'll think about it. Where you taking me this time? To swim with the dolphins?"

"I could if you wanted me to." He released her and opened the door to the passenger side of his car. He watched her get in and flashed his smile when she caught him stare at her backside once again.

It was barely eleven a.m. when they arrived back at Cindy's home. Kofi parked on the street and escorted her to the front door. He refused to simply drop her off. What would it take for him to lose the good guy act? Alonzo pulled the door open the moment they reached the front steps.

"Hello, Mr. Miller," Kofi said.

"Call me Alonzo, Kofi."

"Yes, sir."

Cindy blew out a breath. Alonzo pulled her into his side and squeezed her nose. "Morning, Ella. Where'd you scurry off to?"

"Kofi took me on a sunrise horse riding date."

"My man," Alonzo said. "Come inside."

Cindy cringed. She wanted a nap, and she wouldn't relax with Kofi in her house. He stole a glance in her direction, then faced her father.

"I'd love to, but your daughter wants her space."

Alonzo paused, then gripped Kofi's hand again. "You know her well," he surmised. "Don't be a stranger."

"Daddy," Cindy sang.

"Oh, you want me to walk away so you can say goodbye?" he teased. "I'll listen from inside."

"No, he won't," Mama Tremaine said from somewhere behind him.

Cindy blushed as her father closed the door.

"Your dad is cool people."

She leaned up and hugged him as she yawned again. "Thanks. Where are we going later? You have to tell me how to dress."

"We're gonna tag along with Felicia to the club. She can get in anywhere, and we don't wait in the line once she tells them we're related and she's not my date."

"I'll think about it," she said as she stepped into the doorframe.

Before Cindy could open the door, Kofi pulled the back of her shirt in his direction. He turned her around and wrapped his arms around her waist. He kissed her and swiped his tongue across her lips.

"Please do."

Cindy gave Kofi a small wave as she reopened then closed the door once she was on the other side. She rested against it and hummed sleepily.

"Your prince took you out this morning?" Dreeyah asked when Cindy bumped into her.

"Kofi?"

"Is he the bald, chocolate one from the wedding? The one you and Stasia need to fight about and get it over with."

Cindy's eyes bulged. Stasia sat on the couch across the room from where they stood.

"You were out with Kofi?" Stasia asked. Her jet-black brows were furrowed, and she crossed her arms.

Cindy nodded. "I can't make up my mind. I keep going back and forth. But today he took me horseback riding."

Stasia grinned. "It's all good, sis. I'll step aside. He ain't that fine."

Cindy yawned for the umpteenth time. "Thank God for that. He wants to take me out again tonight."

She leaned in her sister's direction and threw up her hand. They high fived.

"You're weird as hell, Cindy." Dreeyah chuckled.

Cindy nodded. "Maybe."

She showered and fantasized about Kofi's hands on her instead of her own. He'd been a gentleman on their date but the right amount of savage at the cabin. How adventurous would he get with her? Could the same man who insisted he walk her to the door tighten his hand around her neck? She was all for Prince Charming, but only if he could handle her.

Cindy applied her after shower oils and dressed in her house clothes. She prayed for a sign before she laid down for a nap. *Is Kofi the one? Or should I keep my options open until he steps up?*

* * *

The white furniture and drapes sprinkled throughout the club gave it a more upscale illusion than it was. Kofi was underwhelmed. It may have been because Cindy wasn't by his side as opposed to the faux opulence of the establishment. She decided she wanted to meet him at the club instead of riding together.

"Seriously, Kofi. Don't stand there with a sour look on your face all night. If the princess blew you off, there's plenty more available."

Felicia waved her hand toward a sea of fine, barely dressed women. He was irritated that he didn't want to pass the time with any of them. Kofi wanted Cynthia Miller. He was a patient man. And instead of wasting a night out, he'd stay and blow off some steam. Besides, he'd made his mark with Cindy once today—that should hold her over until next time.

Kofi checked his watch and found it was close to one a.m. He moseyed across the club and ordered an overpriced drink at the bar. As he waited for the bartender to return, a pair of small, soft hands covered his eyes. She came after all.

"Tamika?" Kofi teased. Cindy's smell was distinct from anyone else's. It was her, and he was sure of it.

Her hands fell. When he turned to face her, she placed them on her hips with sass. The fitted dress fastened around her neck and exposed the skin on her back and arms. The gold color complemented her complexion, and the short length taunted him.

"Who?"

"Damn," Kofi muttered. Other than his swear, he was speechless. She wore the hell out of her clothes.

"Tamika, huh?"

"You sounded like someone I know," he lied. If he had things his way, he would be respectful, yet cut to the chase. Cindy wanted rough and abstract. She was turned on by the game of cat and mouse, and Kofi would oblige... for now.

Her eyes searched his. "Who is Tamika?"

"I thought that was your fine ass," Dante bellowed from behind Cindy. He wrapped his hands around her waist, and Kofi cringed. *The hell he got his hands on her like that for? Buddy's acting real familiar. Did they come here together?*

"Dante. Hey," she said and wiggled out of his grip.

"Come here." He didn't ask.

Dante guided her to the dance floor through a sea of people. Kofi could easily see Cindy's signature red hair. She could see him too. With his jaw clenched, he shifted his body and leaned against the bar to face them.

Cindy danced a safe distance from Dante until another man showed interest. Dante pulled her closer, and when she noticed the vein in Kofi's head, she rolled her hips. It was like homecoming all over again. This time, they wouldn't be interrupted. Not only would Cindy leave with him tonight; he would seal the deal.

She was his girl; she just didn't know it yet. Despite the fire in his belly, he smiled at her when she backed it up on Dante while she checked to make sure Kofi could see. Cindy wasn't pressed over this fool. In fact, she was annoyed when he appeared out of nowhere.

His legs were extended in front of him, and a petite woman stumbled over them. Her platform heel tilted, and she would have fallen had Kofi not caught her.

"Oh my, thank you," she said when he placed her upright.

"It's not a problem."

She extended her hand, and he accepted it. The small woman

was beautiful, and since Cindy was with Dante again, a friendly conversation wouldn't be a big deal. "I'm Gabrielle."

"Kofi."

She paused and took him in.

"Kofi Carter?"

"Yeah. Do I know you?"

"You sat next to me in Algebra for an entire year in high school. I had glasses and braces though," she admitted.

"Gabby Wabby?"

She narrowed her eyes and slapped his arm playfully. "Nobody's called me that in years."

"How have you been? You look good."

"Huh?" she asked with her hand cupped at her ear. The music shifted, making the background noise increase.

He leaned down near her ear and repeated, "How have you been? You look good!"

"Thanks." She blushed. "I'm only in town for the weekend. How about you?"

"I stayed."

She turned her small body, so she rested against the bar and faced him fully. "What have you been up to? What do you do?"

"Remember how much I liked animals?"

"Yeah. You and your fine ass brothers lived on a farm, right?"

He nodded. He was always singled out as the most handsome of his siblings. *If she says Dev and Maurice are fine, is she feeling me?*

"I always had a crush on you."

His eyes widened. "For real?"

"Yes."

"I became a vet."

"Really?" She squealed. She leaned in and gave him a congratulatory hug. She pressed her breasts into him when she did.

"Hey, baby. Who is this?" Cindy asked. She rested in the crook of Kofi's shoulder and silently announced he was off-limits. When had she finished her dance? And where the hell was Dante?

"This is Gabrielle. We went to school together," Kofi offered. He gave them both a big smile. "This is Cindy."

Gabby extended her hand, but the fiery red head beside him left it suspended there. "It was nice catching up with you, Kofi Carter. Call me some time," she insisted as she sashayed away from them.

"He won't!" Cindy spat.

Tickled, Kofi gazed down at her. "Cynthia Miller, that was mean."

She crossed her arms. The pout on her face was almost as sexy as her territorial display toward Gabby. "That's what you like? Stick thin girls with stripper shoes?"

"You jealous?"

Cindy rolled her eyes and attempted to put space between them. Kofi grasped her so she couldn't move.

"No," she lied.

"How you think I feel when every time I look up, Dante has a handful of your ass?"

She put her hands on her hips and faced him. "You like it, Kofi! I saw the way you stared at me."

"You think I like it when you tease me? The shit drives me crazy, girl."

His voice had risen three octaves. A very small part of him could admit he enjoyed the rush. He leaned in to kiss her when his phone vibrated. She was so close that she felt it too.

"Is that stripper shoes?" Cindy sassed.

He pulled out his phone to check. "Nah, it's Felicia. She knows better than to come somewhere with me then leave without telling me. Walk out to the front with me. I need to see whoever this old ass dude is first. Then we leavin'."

Cindy nodded and followed him. He grabbed her hand, and she took it willingly. Cindy crashed into the back of him when an older man bumped into him. Unlike Cindy's dyed hair, this man was a natural ginger with freckles sprinkled across his cheeks. It was strange because the woman he dragged with him was familiar. Her eyes were covered with dark glasses, and were it not for their ages, Kofi would have assumed the woman was semi-famous.

"What happened?" Cindy asked from behind him.

"Sorry. Some old man having an affair bumped into me."

She grinned. Cindy was a freak, and he was sick to death of their always interrupted, cat and mouse dynamic. He would be knee-deep in her guts before the night was over.

"You didn't have to come out front," Felicia whined.

"Yeah, I did." Kofi damn near broke the man's hand he squeezed it so hard when he introduced himself. "Kofi Carter. And you are?"

The man was in his early forties. He wasn't as old as Kofi expected. This was a change for Felicia who typically went for recently divorced fifty-year-old men. When Cindy stepped from behind Kofi, she shrieked.

"Uncle David?"

"Hey, Ella," the man said.

Now that she'd said it, recognition covered Kofi's features. This was Alonzo's brother. He and Felicia must have exchanged numbers at the wedding.

"Lonzo know you here? Wearing that?"

"Don't change the subject, Uncle David."

"I'm grown," he added and smoothed his eyebrows.

Kofi released a throaty laugh. "Well, you kids have a wonderful time," he said to Felicia and gave a hard pat to David's back.

Felicia's face flushed, and she swatted Kofi's arm before she stormed off with Cindy's uncle a few steps behind her.

"I can't believe him. I'm telling my dad." Cindy pouted.

"Let's go." Kofi stared down at her. He tipped her chin up until his lips connected with hers.

"That's how it is, Cindy?" Dante asked from a few feet away.

Cindy opened her mouth, but Kofi put his hand up to stop her.

"Whatever you had with her is over! She's been using you to make me jealous, and it worked. This my lady now," Kofi said. He didn't look to Cindy for confirmation. This was the first time he was sure she agreed. Enough was enough.

Dante stepped forward in Cindy's direction but was cut off by Kofi. "I said she's done." He pulled out a piece of gum as if he wasn't threatened at all. Dante's eyes bounced from Cindy to Kofi. When he caught Kofi's death glare, he sucked his teeth and turned to re-enter the club.

* * *

It was about damn time Kofi took charge. He'd called her out for using Dante to make him jealous. What took her by surprise was how he let her do it. She had to admit, she was relieved not to have to break things off with Dante. Kofi had done it for her.

In every love story, there was always a battle for the leading lady, and Kofi showed her she was his. Her center pulsed, seeing him in action.

"I wanna pack a bag first," she said as Kofi fastened his seat belt.

Kofi stilled. "You staying all night with me?"

She nodded.

He flashed her his chip-toothed smile and peeled out of the parking lot. "Dr. Carter, what has gotten into you?"

He laid his hand across her thighs. "The question is, how you gonna handle when I get into you?"

He watched as her eyes closed, and she threw her head back. At the rate they went, she wouldn't make it home or wherever they were headed. She was tempted to beg him to pull over to release her pent-up sexual frustration. As he drove, she pulled his hand between her legs. His fingers rubbed against her center.

She moaned before his hand even touched her bare flesh. Kofi was skilled enough to elicit a reaction without moving her panties.

"I don't know if I can wait much longer," he admitted.

"Me either."

He finally pushed past her panties and released a throaty moan of his own when he discovered how wet she was.

"You heard me say you was my lady?"

She nodded.

Kofi slid a finger inside of her as he smoothly drove through the night traffic. "You my lady, Cindy? I wanna hear you say it."

"I don't know."

He slid two fingers inside. "You don't?"

She shook her head. He could toy with her until she came. Cindy wouldn't willingly tell him what he wanted to hear. She didn't operate like that.

Kofi's movement stilled.

With her eyes closed and her head back, she said, "Don't stop. Please don't stop."

He removed his hand completely, and her eyes flew open. She turned to face him. "Of course, I'm your lady, Kofi. Why did you stop?"

His mouth was wide open. "Baby, something's wrong."

Cindy shifted her focus from the frustrating bald man of hers to the windshield. There were no sirens, just lights. They danced around and decorated their faces with red, white, and blue. Something *was* wrong. Someone was hurt. But who?

Chapter Seven

It was like the movie, *A Soul's Unrest: The Haunting of Damon Daniels*. Why hadn't anyone called her? Stasia was a bumbling mess. Cindy could hear her wails, while Dreeyah was quiet. She was always detached, but now her expression was completely numb.

Cindy couldn't move her legs fast enough. They were weighed down like they were made of lead. That was when she saw the black bag on the gurney.

"Daddy?" she called out. Where was he? Had something terrible happened to Mama Tremaine? How the hell would she help him through yet another loss of a spouse?

When Mama Tremaine followed the paramedic from the house, Cindy's legs gave out. Someone caught her. Kofi?

"Where's my dad?" she yelled. No one needed to tell her he was in the bag.

"Cindy Ella," Mama Tremaine wailed.

"Let me see," she demanded of the paramedic. A man with orange hair and freckles nodded to the employee, and he did as she asked.

Alonzo Miller's face was serene. There looked to be no struggle. Maybe he hadn't seen it coming. *What the hell happened? He was just here.*

Cindy unzipped the bag further. She placed her face against his and wept. The gray stubble on his cheeks was still warm, but he was gone. There was no doubt in her mind about that.

"Daddy, how could you?" she shrieked. "You promised you wouldn't leave. You promised!"

Cindy went from hugging to punching her father's lifeless body. Kofi pulled her to him because she wouldn't let go. She'd all but yanked him from the gurney. Where she got the strength was a mystery. Mama Tremaine was at their side.

They looked down at him like they were at a funeral. Cindy went through a phase—as an adolescent—where she was obsessed with death. Everything that died had to have a ceremony and a burial. She snuck into a funeral home once and fell asleep. Her father couldn't find her for hours.

When he confronted her about it, she said it brought her closer to her mom. What was she supposed to do now? Thoughts of Leena's warning crowded her overwhelmed mind. She should have taken her words to heart. She never did say goodbye. Mama Tremaine had even suggested she get alone time with him. Cindy never took advantage of the motherly suggestion.

A new wave of emotion hit Cindy. Her legs gave out again. Had Kofi not been behind her, she would have fallen to the concrete sidewalk.

"Daddy!"

The paramedic zipped up the bag and wheeled him away. Cindy tried to go with him, but everyone insisted it was better if she didn't since he was long gone. Her colorful world turned gray. No longer could she hear the birds sing, nor could she see the beauty in the great outdoors that she adored.

Love wasn't enough. Love took the biggest loss today. For the first time in her life, love was nowhere. What was the fucking point?

* * *

Sudden cardiac death. She googled the cause of death incessantly. It got to the point where Mama Tremaine threatened to confiscate her devices. Cindy was obsessed. She was fixated on the idea that the doctor had gotten it wrong. From her research, she learned it was extremely rare.

Cindy had put immense pressure on her father to visit the doctor regularly for this very reason. She didn't want to be alone. He complied, although he swore up and down, he would meet his grand-children and possibly their children. Cindy chuckled to herself about that conversation. He was only willing to stick around for his great grands if he still had all his bodily functions.

Missing him was an understatement. She lost a limb. It was as though someone reached inside of her chest and ripped fragments of it out. She hadn't spoken in weeks. She didn't have shit to say. Her father was taken from her at the end of May. The last time she checked, it was almost August.

She couldn't remember her father's funeral. Her body went, but her spirit was somewhere else. When they spoke about the future and he made her sign estate papers, they agreed his homegoing would be a celebration of life. But under the circumstances, that notion had been put on the back burner. Cindy was barely lucid most days.

She'd been prescribed an antidepressant. It wasn't good for her, because when she was on them, she had no feelings. She was in a dangerous position and would need to let someone know soon. If she kept on, she would have no will to live. Too many times, she considered how much better it would be if she joined Celina and Alonzo Miller for good. They could finally be a happy family again.

Her search engine history would get her a one-way ticket to a white jacket. She was sure he hadn't gone peacefully. Alonzo Miller was murdered. She was certain. And it wasn't grieving. This was different.

"Princess," Dreeyah sang. At least she attempted to sing. Her harsh, low voice hurt Cindy's ears.

She slammed her laptop and stared beyond Dreeyah. She didn't want to see anyone. Cindy didn't have the strength.

"You have another visitor."

Professor Brenton, her fairy godmother, floated into Cindy's room and brought a light and energy with her Cindy's soul desperately needed. *How did she know to visit now?* Her uncle David and a few of her classmates stopped by to see her, but those visits dwindled. Kofi called and texted and had even sent flowers. At that, she smiled. Kofi was not a flowers and card type of man, so for him to send them, she must have been special.

"Cynthia, sweetheart. I'm so, so sorry," Brenton whispered.

Cindy hadn't looked at herself and only showered when Mama Tremaine physically walked her in. Her hair was unkempt. She could see her thick curves had dwindled. Not because she willingly stuck to a diet, but because she lost her appetite a month ago.

Tears filled Cindy's eyes. She hadn't cried in weeks. The medicine made sure of it. Her tears at the sight of her fairy godmother weren't a result of sorrow, but a deep gratitude for the woman's presence in her life and in her time of need.

Brenton sat beside Cindy and pulled her into a deep embrace. Mama Tremaine hugged Cindy too, but after her father was gone, it was different. They both were... distant. He was the only reason they were in each other's lives, and now he was gone. Brenton was there out of concern. She was at Cindy's side by choice.

Cindy wasn't sure how long they sat that way. It was long enough for Cindy to drift off to sleep.

"Cynthia."

Cindy lifted from the woman's chest and wiped her eyes.

"They tell me you haven't spoken."

Cindy lowered her head. It wasn't that she didn't have anything *meaningful* to say. She was convinced they wouldn't listen or, worse, they would have her committed.

"Tell me. You can tell me."

"He..."

Brenton removed her shoes and sat cross legged on Cindy's large bed. She waited patiently for Cindy's response as if she had all the time in the world.

"He was murdered. I know he was."

Professor Brenton's eyes widened. "Are you safe here?" she whispered. She looked from Cindy to the slightly opened bedroom.

Cindy nodded. She wasn't sure of the motive, but her father didn't die from sudden cardiac arrest. She and his cardiologist had met. He said her father had the heart of a thirty-year-old and could date someone her age if he wanted. They both got a kick out of it.

"What do you need?"

Cindy shrugged. "I don't know." Tears fell from her eyes again.

"Stay with me tonight. A change in environment might do you some good."

Cindy stood. She went to her dresser to gather some of her things.

"What are you doing?" Brenton asked with concern laced in her tone.

"Packing a bag."

* * *

The interns started at the hospital August twenty-second, just as his mini-me informed him during orientation. Every time Kofi saw them, his heart ached. It was the second week of September now, and Cindy still wasn't there. She lost her father over the summer, and he'd never been more powerless. He couldn't help her with this. Other than social media, he hadn't seen her since the funeral.

She hugged him after the service. And for a moment, he saw a glimpse of the old Cindy. She let him press a quick peck to her lips with no concern for what anyone else at the church would say. She wasn't completely gone, but she was buried deep underneath what was likely grief. Kofi had never lost anyone close to him. He didn't know how grief worked.

From what he read, people grieved differently. Though he wanted to be near her and hold her through her pain, the right thing to do was to give her time.

"Where's the red head?" Johns asked, interrupting Kofi's thoughts.

Kofi huffed and stood. "She had a death in her family."

"That's too bad. I was looking forward to watching you train yourself," Johns joked. "You check up on her?"

It was a good question. He hadn't. Not really. He'd given her the space he assumed she needed. Kofi patted Johns on the shoulder and left the cafeteria.

"Where are you going?" he directed at Kofi's back.

"I'm taking the rest of the day off."

Kofi took long strides and was in his car in no time. Maybe she didn't want space. He had no idea where his mind would be if he lost either of his parents. The only way he could know how Cindy was would be if he laid eyes on her himself.

Kofi parked on the street in front of her home and dragged in a deep breath. There was a slight chill in the air that wasn't a result of the pending fall season. Kofi admired Alonzo Miller. He missed him and wasn't sure he'd accepted the kind man was gone until this moment. No longer was the area crowded with medical professionals and their vehicles like earlier in the summer when he and Cindy arrived.

The street was eerily quiet. An all-black car approached. It came out of nowhere like maybe it had been parked on the street. When the driver passed Kofi, he saw it was the same ginger-haired man who he'd seen with the mysterious woman the night at the club. He made eye contact with Kofi but didn't bother to wave or acknowledge him at all. Maybe he lived in the housing division with Cindy.

Kofi whipped out his phone and opted to text Cindy of his presence.

Kofi: I'm outside
Cindy: outside where

Relief washed over him. She'd returned his message within moments. Hopefully she was here and willing to see him.

Kofi: at your front door. I want to see you, Cindy
Cindy: okay

Moments later, the door crept open. Even with what looked like a noticeable drop in her weight, Cindy was breathtaking. He surveyed her from head to toe as if to ensure she was truly there and that she was fine. His prior urge to claim her for selfish purposes was replaced in an instant. Kofi wanted to protect Cindy now. He would make sure he gave her anything *she* needed.

"Hey," she said. There was a small smile across her blemish-free face.

He grabbed her hand and gently tugged her from the door, so she stepped outside with him. She went willingly. Cindy closed the door behind her and lifted her head to see him. He hugged her tight and relaxed when she melted into him.

"You smell good," she said with the side of her face resting against his chest.

"Is that right?"

She pulled back and stared up at him. "Yes, Dr. Carter."

He grinned down at her. "I missed you."

She separated her body from his. If he was honest, he wished she hadn't. But he'd follow her lead. Whatever she was comfortable with was what they would do.

"I missed you too, Kofi. I've wanted to call you, but..." Her voice trailed off.

"Take a walk with me."

She nodded and followed him without hesitation.

They started their walk in her neighborhood in silence. The leaves were multi-colored on the trees and ground. It hadn't quite become jacket weather, but it would be in no time.

"I want to ask you something, but I'm afraid to sound ignorant."

She grasped his hand and intertwined their fingers. It was a small gesture that went a long way.

"How are you, Cindy?"

They continued to walk. Cindy looked down at their feet while Kofi observed her every move.

"I... I know everyone assumes I can't accept what happened, but it's not that."

Kofi stroked her fingers to show his support.

She took her time and finally said, "It wasn't a fluke or natural cause."

Her refusal to accept Alonzo's passing was one of the five stages of grief. It was expected and perfectly normal. He wouldn't tell her that though. He would be a safe space for her to process however she chose.

"Tell me more," he urged. The last thing Kofi wanted to do was to pretend to be her doctor. But they were the only supportive words that came to mind.

She pulled her fingers from his and faced him on the trail where they stood at the side of her neighborhood. "My dad was murdered."

Kofi's expression was unreadable when the words fell from her mouth. She hadn't intended to tell him, but she was safe when he was around. The only other time she felt that way was when she was with Professor Brenton. Cindy stayed with her for a few days. She eventually returned home because the answers she needed were in that house.

If it were up to her, that would be the last place she slept. It was hard to pass his and Mama Tremaine's room. That was where it happened.

"Why do you think that?"

She shrugged. How could she explain that she felt it in her gut?

She didn't have concrete evidence, but she was sure he hadn't passed peacefully in his sleep. "I know I sound crazy."

Cindy turned to continue their walk. The movement and time outdoors were good for her. She could admit that Kofi and his energy were good for her too.

"I didn't say you sound crazy. I asked why you think that," he reiterated.

"It's like this movie I watched, *A Soul's Unrest: The Haunting of Damon Daniels*."

Kofi's eyes widened. He'd seen it. His brothers were obsessed with those types of movies. "The one where her son killed her and was haunted until he fessed up?"

"Yes!"

"Someone you know killed Alonzo?"

She nodded. Her eyes were fixed on the rocks in their path. If she wasn't careful, she would end up in a psychiatric ward.

"Why do you think that, baby?" he asked again.

Cindy appreciated Kofi's gentleness with her. She couldn't imagine what she would say if the roles were reversed. "I can't let myself fully grieve until I figure out what happened to my dad. His spirit won't rest until I do. I know that sounds weird but... And my roommates—"

"Mama Tremaine and your sisters?"

"Yeah, them. They aren't grieving."

"What do you mean?"

She stopped again and peered up at him. "I can't put my finger on it, but they're acting guilty, especially Mama Tremaine."

He searched her eyes and used his hand to sweep her unruly hair from her cheek. She hadn't bothered to tame it. "That doesn't sound crazy at all. I am worried though."

Cindy's stomach twisted. What if Kofi told someone what she said?

"About you staying there, Cindy. If any of them were involved, how safe could it be for you to be sleeping there every night?"

It was exactly what her fairy godmother said when she told her. Neither of them called her crazy or irrational. They were immediately concerned with her safety if her gut feeling told her someone in that house was involved in her father's death.

A weak smile flashed across her lips, and water filled her eyes. "Thank you, Kofi."

"For what?"

A single tear escaped her eye. He used the pad of his thumb to brush it away. Cindy leaned up and kissed the corner of his mouth. "For believing me. And for being concerned."

He returned her smile and draped his long arm around her neck, pulling her body into his.

"Did I ever tell you how fine you look in scrubs?" she asked, changing the subject.

He released a hearty laugh, and the sound vibrated through her body. She wished she could crawl into him and retreat from the world. It was wishful thinking. The fight in her spirit wouldn't let her rest until her father could. He deserved to truly be at peace. But as it stood, there were too many loose ends for that.

He pulled her even closer and planted a kiss on her forehead. "You haven't. That's why I came to visit. I missed seeing you in yours."

She tilted her head upward.

"The other interns started. Even Johns asked about you."

Another tear fell from her eye, although she chuckled. "He did?"

"Yep. He said something about wishing he could see me have to figure out how to train an intern just like me."

Cindy laughed. "There's nothing wrong with initiative."

"Is that what you call it?" He laughed again, and it was the most therapeutic sound. "I gave Johns gray hair, the little he has left. You, Cynthia Miller, will have him as bald as me."

She beamed. "It's nice to see you. I thought about you a lot these last months. I been meaning to tell you—"

The ringing of her phone interrupted her mid-sentence. She

retrieved it from the pocket of her sweats and sighed when she saw the caller.

"Everything okay?" Kofi asked.

"It's Dreeyah. I don't wanna talk to her." Cindy accepted the call anyway. "What's up?"

She placed the phone on speaker as if it was simply too intimate to hear the voice in her ear. Kofi didn't mind. He was attentive to whatever she needed at that point.

"Hey. Sorry to bother you. I saw you stepped out with your prince," she said in her typical flat tone. There was a sadness in her voice that hadn't been there while Alonzo was around. It was clear Dreeyah liked him more than she did other humans.

Kofi's thick eyebrows flew up. Cindy gave him a sheepish grin. He pointed at himself. "I'm the prince?"

She nodded.

"It's fine. What's going on?"

"There's somebody here to see you," Dreeyah uttered.

Irritation filled Cindy's body. "If it's not Professor Brenton, I'm not interested. I don't have the bandwidth for peopling," she said.

"Is that your fairy godmother?" Kofi asked. He did a horrible job hiding his playful grin.

She swatted him and nodded.

"It's a detective. He says he wants to speak with you," Dreeyah added.

Cindy's mouth fell open. This was a sign. Finally, someone who didn't have any attachment to the situation would hear her concerns. Her father deserved justice, and she would see to it that he got it.

They were quiet on the walk back to Cindy's home. She couldn't calm her nerves in anticipation of this meeting. Professor Brenton urged her to talk to the police. She did, but after they made her wait for hours, they rushed the conversation because her father's death wasn't identified as suspicious. Why was there a detective at her home if that was the case?

"How can I help?" Kofi asked. His voice was tender and throaty.

It reminded her of all the close calls they'd shared. Her mind and her heart were focused on the task at hand, but her body sure piped up about its needs whenever Kofi was around.

"Will you stay with me while we talk?"

"If that will make you comfortable, absolutely."

Chapter Eight

"I'm Detective Landry," the man with the ginger-colored hair said as he reached his hand toward Cindy.

Kofi recognized the black car parked in front of Cindy's home. He'd seen it less than an hour ago when he first arrived. Maybe that was why this same man had been there. And maybe that was why he'd tried, but failed, at discretion early this summer at the club.

"Cynthia Miller?"

"Just Cindy, please," Cindy said as she accepted his hand.

Mama Tremaine brought a tray of tea into the living room.

"Hello, Kofi," she said when she entered. Her hands shook when she hovered over the table.

"Hello, Mrs. Miller. Let me get that for you," Kofi offered.

Detective Landry cleared his throat.

"Thank you, son," she said sweetly and scurried out of the room.

It was weird, even to Kofi. While he didn't have first-hand experience with grief, her behavior was bizarre. Cindy was right. She acted guilty. Had she been involved in Alonzo's passing? Was she afraid the detective would find out?

Stasia walked past the living room area but didn't speak. He hadn't seen Dreeyah at all. A chill ran up his spine. *What the hell is going on here?*

Cindy took one of the mugs and smelled it. Instead of grabbing a tea bag, she set it back down. He noticed and so did the detective. Was Cindy afraid Mama Tremaine put something harmful in her tea?

"Landry?" Kofi asked. "Is that creole?"

The olive-hued man clenched his jaw then responded, "It is." He studied Kofi and asked, "Are you the boyfriend?"

He was prepared to state he was her friend since they hadn't discussed a relationship after her father passed, but Cindy cut in. "Yes. I'd like him to stay while we talk. Will that be an issue?"

Kofi tried to conceal his illation when she said they were a couple. She may have simply wanted to get to the heart of the visit, but it affected him, nonetheless. He shifted and adjusted his scrubs. This was not about him; it was about Cindy's father.

"Not at all. I'll get right to it. I got word at the station that you have reason to believe your father's passing wasn't due to natural causes. Is that correct?"

Cindy ran her hands through her hair. She breathed deeply while Kofi studied the detective. Did Landry remember him from the club? He didn't know any detectives personally, but his behavior was as strange as the women in the house. Maybe it was a coincidence that Kofi saw him, then he was assigned to this case.

"Correct."

"Did something happen before or after he passed to give you this idea? Did you stumble across anything?"

"My father was a healthy man. He was also very wealthy. I got paperwork from the estate attorney that he left me everything."

Kofi's eyes swung in Cindy's direction. It was odd. He'd married Mama Tremaine and had two bonus daughters that he loved dearly. Kofi expected Cindy would get the most, but Alonzo didn't seem like the type who wouldn't plan for his future or completely exclude his new family members.

The detective cleared his throat. "Does that surprise you?"

"Yes. After he got married, he told me that he'd leave the business and the investments to me, but..."

Kofi grabbed her hand to show his support.

"But he said he'd divided his savings three ways between his new wife and daughters. Somewhere between February and the summer, he changed it back. It doesn't make sense. Unless... unless he had a reason not to trust them."

Cindy's eyes were fierce and laser focused. She hadn't referred to Tremaine as Mama Tremaine, and she didn't call Dreeyah and Stasia her bonus sisters. *What the hell is going on?*

"Could any of them have known about this?" the detective continued.

Kofi didn't trust him. He couldn't put his finger on why. It was more than their run-ins. This interview was too personal.

Cindy considered his question. "It's possible."

Detective Landry received an alert on his phone. Kofi studied the man. He had a poker face. Because Kofi's eyes were on him, he cleared his throat. The detective moved to the front of his seat as if the interview had come to an end.

"There's one other thing," Cindy added. "She may have been cheating."

Kofi's eyes darted to Cindy's. She stared out of the window. Sadness draped over her shoulders like an invisible cloak.

Landry cleared his throat again.

"You need some water, man?" Kofi asked. *If this shady mutha-fucka clears his throat one more time. What the hell is his problem?*

Landry cut his eyes at Kofi, but Kofi was steadfast in his position. Cindy unraveled before him. First, Cindy spoke of grief. Then she divulged her concern of foul play. Now, she admitted her belief that Mama Tremaine had an affair, and this beady eyed bastard has a frog in his throat.

"I'm fine," he said and redirected his gaze to Cindy.

"What makes you think she was cheating? They were newly married, correct?"

"Yes. But, after my father… was taken from me, I had a lot of time to think. As far back as the wedding planning, Mama Tremaine showed a lot of care toward my father. She loved him, or so it seemed. But she made one too many secret phone calls."

"How so?"

"I thought maybe she was planning for the wedding. Only, I did most of the work. And it wasn't just that she spoke to unidentified people; it was the way she did it."

There was a thump in the next room. All heads flew in the direction of the kitchen.

"Sorry, I dropped my bag," Stasia volunteered.

"It's not a good idea for her to have this conversation here," Kofi interjected.

Detective Landry sighed. "No one has been accused of anything. I'm simply gathering information."

His blood boiled. "She's telling you her father's money may be linked to his death while she's in the house with people who may have an interest in said money, and you think it's safe to gather information where anyone could hear?"

Cindy grabbed his arm because he, too, had scooted to the edge of his seat. He'd taken on the role to ensure Cindy was covered. If the law wouldn't do it, he could handle it himself. And as far as he was concerned, this conversation was no longer safe.

"We could always do this at the station. I doubt Cindy would want that," he offered.

Under any other circumstance, Kofi would have fallen in line. Landry was the professional, after all, but this was different. Kofi was pissed at how little effort this man put into the entire process.

Kofi observed Cindy for long moments. "Are you okay?" he asked her in a hushed tone. It was obvious Detective Landry could still hear him, but if anyone stood outside of the room, they couldn't. "Do you want to keep talking to him?"

She nodded. "That's the main thing. The change in my father's money, her inappropriate conversations, and…" Cindy chewed on her lip. She returned her eyes toward the window. It was where the wedding took place. There was no way she was at peace here. "With the exception of Dreeyah, they don't act like they miss him. They act like they're hiding something."

"What do you mean inappropriate conversations?" Landry pressed.

"Flirting. She flirted on the phone."

"How can you be sure she wasn't talking to a cousin or a girl-friend?" he queried.

"Because when I talk to Kofi, I couldn't hide my blush if I tried."

Kofi relaxed his clenched jaw and winked at Cindy. She had him all over the place. One minute, he wanted to whisk her out of there, and the next, he was completely smitten and convinced he could endure anything if she was near him.

"There's a glow a woman has when she speaks to a man she's romantically involved with. I noticed at the time, but I didn't want to see."

"What do you mean?" he asked.

That was when her tears returned. "I was so desperate to experience the love of a mother, I overlooked what was in my face the whole time. Maybe he confronted her and threatened to leave." Cindy shrugged.

"That's enough for now," Detective Landry said as he stood. "Give me a call if anything else comes up. I'll do the same." He handed her a business card. "Thank you for sharing everything you did. It couldn't have been easy."

Kofi still didn't trust him. If there was an opportunity for Cindy to get a different detective, he'd be the first to insist she did.

* * *

After her talk with Detective Landry, Cindy didn't want Kofi to leave. He must have had work since he wore scrubs, but she was able to breathe much better in his presence.

"Would you stay?"

Kofi craned his neck and surveyed his surroundings. It was creepy as hell there. If he had his own place, he would demand she left with him right away, but he didn't. He lived with his parents and his immature brothers.

He nodded. "I don't have anywhere else I need to be."

She tugged on his scrub top. "Not even the hospital?"

"Nah, I told them I was leaving for the day. I couldn't stand seeing the other interns."

They'd sat on the sofa where the interview had taken place. She shifted her body to face him.

"You missed me bad, huh?" she teased.

"I told you I did. What are you gonna do now? Before you answer, is there somewhere private we can talk?"

"Yeah. Upstairs."

She stood and grabbed his hand. They had to pass the kitchen to get to the side of the house with the bedrooms. Tremaine had a dish and towel in her hand. Cindy stared at her but said nothing.

Kofi waved, but Cindy didn't give him time to make small talk. On their way up the stairs, she saw Gus.

"Who is this?" Kofi asked. Cindy saw a twinkle in his eye that only fellow animal lovers held.

"This my boyfriend, Gus," Cindy crooned.

Gus walked past Cindy and allowed Kofi to hold and pet him. "Your boyfriend, huh?"

Cindy rolled her eyes. "You're such a thot, Gus. You just gon' forget who found you and took you in?" she teased.

They reached the second level, but Cindy pointed up once again.

"Your room is up there?" he asked, his tone a mixture of confusion and concern.

"She hides up there," Stasia spat. She entered the hallway while Kofi held Gus.

"Hey, Stasia," Kofi said. He walked in her direction to say hello, but Gus hissed.

"Gus," Cindy tried, but Gus jumped down and scurried away. He'd done this on more than one occasion with her, yet he hadn't hesitated with Kofi.

"I don't hide up there. Y'all swear you're allergic to my cat," Cindy countered.

"Whatever, Cindy," Stasia said and disappeared into one of the rooms. She didn't acknowledge Kofi at all.

Cindy turned to the second set of steps and ascended them with slumped shoulders.

"It's actually really nice up here," Kofi said, relieved once they were fully in the room.

The ceiling and walls were white which brightened the space. The dark stained hardwood floors and furniture balanced the decor. A queen-sized bed comfortably fit on the third level in addition to a built-in reading nook next to a large window and two recliners.

"You thought I was banished to a dusky attic by my evil step-mother and stepsisters," she teased. She chuckled, but her eyes maintained a sadness that only let up when she was with Gus, Brenton, or Kofi.

"I did," he admitted. Kofi sat on the loveseat across from her bed. "So, technically, you have two rooms?"

"I have seven rooms. My father left this house to me. They know it, and so do I."

"About that... Now that I know they didn't get any money, what's your plan as far as your living arrangements? Your current setup isn't safe. People go to all kinds of lengths to survive."

"I *have* to stay here. It's the only way I'm going to figure out what happened. I should have listened to Leena. Maybe I could ask her to fill in the missing blanks."

"Who?" Kofi opened his long legs and made himself comfortable in her space. It distracted her, and she hadn't hidden it well. She was met with a sexy, chipped-tooth smile. He lifted from his relaxed position and rested his elbows on his knees. *Damn this man is fine!*

"Ummm. What?"

"I asked about Leena. You said you should have listened to her. Who is she?"

Flustered from Kofi's good looks and full of trepidation to admit how Leena was relevant, Cindy plopped down on her bed. "I have overshared so much already. You have your own stuff going on. Ask me something else."

Kofi grinned. "Fine. I'm your boyfriend?"

Cindy grabbed a pillow and covered her face. "Not that question," she mumbled. Her words were muted because her mouth was concealed.

Kofi walked toward her bed and kneeled beside it. "I would get in with you, but I don't wanna ruin your bed with my outside clothes," he confessed. "You can answer either. Doesn't matter to me."

She peeked an eye from under her hiding place.

"Damn you're cute," he said as he confiscated the pillow.

"Thank you." Cindy put her gaze everywhere except on Kofi. "Leena is a little girl I met at one of my princess gigs."

She looked over to find a broad smile on Kofi's handsome face.

"What is a princess gig?"

"I swore I told you about this already. I dress up as a princess, and I do princess parties for children."

"Wow. You were created for that job. Continue."

"Anyway, a few months ago, I met a little girl named Leena who scared the shit out of me. My princess name is Ginger, but she came right up to me and called me Cindy."

"Maybe she overheard the adults say your name."

"They refer to me as Ginger too."

"That's your stage name? Ginger?"

She leaned forward and pushed him. "It just made sense to separate myself as a character from that world. So, no one called me

Cindy. It wasn't just that. She told me she knows things. Leena introduced herself as Oya but said her parents named her Leena."

"The fuck?"

"Exactly. It gets worse."

Kofi shivered. "This shit is eerie as hell."

"Who you telling? She said Alonzo was going to be getting out of his body soon."

The door creaked open, and they both jumped. It was Gus.

"Gus, you scared me," Cindy said. She grabbed him and brought him back to her bed. He let Kofi and Cindy take turns petting him. It took the chill out of the air.

"She said he would join Celina. Celina is my mother."

Kofi's eyes bucked. "I see why you don't think he passed away randomly. What else did her weird ass say?"

"In hindsight, the child is quite gifted. If I wasn't afraid her parents would report me, I'd ask her what I'm missing. She said I needed to say goodbye to him like she said goodbye to her gram."

"Damn."

"I know."

"When we going to see her?" he asked.

* * *

Kofi considered himself a brave and confident person. He was up for most challenges. Still, he never wanted to run as bad as he did when he and Cindy arrived at Leena's home. After they spoke at her place, Cindy made a few calls and contacted Leena's mother to coordinate a time and place for the meeting. The chill in the fall air added to the already spooky vibe he got from her neighborhood. The deep, dark gray sky contradicted the fact that it was afternoon.

"You ready?" Cindy asked when he parked in front of the house that matched the address she was given.

He wasn't, but he nodded his head anyway. It had been a few days since Cindy's conversation with Detective Landry. While she weighed whether she would reach back out for his help, she decided to take matters in her own hands. When she asked if Kofi would go with her, he agreed. Now that they were here, he had major reservations.

"She killed a dog?" he asked before Cindy opened the door. His head was a jumbled mess.

Cindy let go of the handle and smiled. "No, baby. She didn't kill a dog. She told another kid that their dog would die. The dog had a pulmonary embolism."

Kofi squirmed in his seat. *What the hell have I gotten myself into?* "You seem calm," he observed.

"I was as freaked out as you are when she spoke to me at the birthday party. I called my dad after because I needed to hear his voice." Cindy blew out a breath and straightened her back. "Things have changed. If she knew he was going to die, maybe she knows what happened. I don't have anything to lose."

Kofi leaned over and pulled her into him. He kissed her cheek and whispered in her ear. "I don't like anything about this little visit, but I'll do whatever you ask if you keep calling me baby."

She angled her head up to him and smiled. "Thank you, baby."

Kofi got out of the car and hustled to Cindy's side to open her door. He'd driven her enough times that she waited to appease him. "Are they expecting us?"

Cindy craned her neck up to take in the enormous colonial style home and nodded. It was overgrown with vines. There were leaves and trees everywhere. She grabbed his hand and steadied her breath.

The stairs that led to the porch creaked when they ascended them. And before Kofi made it on the porch, the door swung open, leaving only a screen door between them.

Cindy reared back and shrieked. "Leena, you scared me."

The little girl waved at them. "Alonzo said he likes Kovi." She giggled then ran in the opposite direction.

Kofi peered down at Cindy and reflexively took a step back. "Shit."

"I know." After a few moments of them watching Leena disappear into the house, Cindy reached out and grabbed the storm door latch.

Fuck, fuck, fuck.

She opened it and went in. Kofi followed her as his eyes darted around the entry.

"Leena," Cindy called out.

"Don't this shit feel like the beginning of a horror flick?" Kofi whispered.

"Hello, you two," a woman who could have been Leena's older clone said.

Cindy shrieked again, and Kofi grabbed his chest. They looked at each other and laughed, although Kofi leaned forward and rested his palms on his knees to catch his breath.

"You must be Cynthia, and you're Kofi." She didn't ask. A chill crept up Kofi's back at the certainty in her voice. Had Cindy told her he was coming in advance? Or was she some kind of freaky psychic like her daughter?

"Did Leena get her gift from you?" Cindy pressed. "I didn't introduce Kofi to either of you."

"Leena's much more advanced in clairaudience than the rest of us."

"Clair who?" Kofi asked with his head on a swivel.

"I'm Leena's mother, Halle, by the way," she said and bowed. "Come on in." Her natural curly hair was parted down the middle and framed her chestnut hued face. Two deep dimples were carved into her otherwise flawless skin.

Cindy and Kofi followed her deeper in the house. There were two steps down in front of a large open space that may have been the living room. It was difficult to tell because there was barely any furniture in the area. Instead, there were many floor pillows that served as meditation seats. The women sat on the cushions, while Kofi stayed a safe distance away and sat on the top stair.

"You've heard of clairvoyance? Essentially seeing future events before they happen?" she asked once they were settled.

"Yes. Is that what Leena has?" Cindy inquired.

"She has the gifts of clairvoyance, clairaudience where she can hear from those who have transitioned, and claircognizance which is a more general knowing."

Kofi's jaw dropped. "What?"

"It's not as bad as it sounds. Cindy here has clairsentience; she just doesn't know it. Or she doesn't trust it. It's those gut feelings she dismisses. Celina had it too. You probably assumed you were simply sensitive or empathic. It's deeper than that if you allow it."

Kofi stood and paced the area near the stairs. He willed himself not to run out of the front door.

"You know my mother too?"

"I feel her energy around you. She is with you now and always. If my family meant you harm, I doubt you would have crossed the threshold."

"Sheesh," Kofi rasped.

Cindy sniffed and wiped her eyes. "I have a gut feeling that someone took my father's life."

"Did Leena tell you that?" Halle asked.

"She predicted he would die soon. Of course, I didn't want to accept it. But now that he has, I'm hoping she can help me with what happened to him. Or at least point me in the right direction with figuring it out."

Before Cindy finished, Leena bopped back into the house from the backyard.

Kofi stilled. "How the hell?"

Cindy and Halle looked at him briefly, then returned their attention to Leena. She took a seat in front of them both. She studied Kofi. "He scared," she announced.

Cindy motioned for him to come sit. "Please, baby."

Sweat beaded on Kofi's brow. "You sure you don't want me to

wait in the car? I don't want to ruin the energy in here with my... reluctance."

"Your spirit is pure. It's good if you stay," Halle insisted.

What the hell am I doing here? Against his better judgment, Kofi went back to the step and took a seat. His head was on a swivel as if he needed to be on guard for whatever came next.

"You believe I know stuff now?" Leena asked. She was an adorable child, despite her creepy abilities. When she looked at someone, it was as though she peered deep into their souls. That was how she regarded Cindy. It was what made her behave wiser than her actual age.

Cindy nodded. "I need help figuring out what happened to him. Can you help me?"

"You scared like Kovi?" she asked. Leena pulled out a box of crayons and a coloring book.

"Kofi," he added from the step.

Leena giggled and colored on the floor.

"A little. I'm more scared not to know who did this. Can you help me, Leena? What really happened?"

"He say the one with the D innocent. She loved him for real."

Cindy focused her attention on Halle. "What does that mean?"

"Sometimes ancestors and spirits communicate with the first letter of someone's name. Anyone in your home's name starts with a D?" Halle asked.

"Dreeyah," Kofi and Cindy said together.

"It's a man Alonzo talking about a lot, a lot," Leena said as she scribbled. She hadn't looked up since she started.

"A man?" Cindy pressed.

"His hair orange."

Kofi shot to his feet again. "Fuck! Landry."

His run-ins with Landry weren't coincidental. He was a shifty man, and the little girl confirmed it.

"What does my dad say about him?" Cindy sniffed.

Kofi's eyes settled on Cindy, and although he wanted nothing more than to bolt through the door, he walked over and took a seat near her. He grabbed her hand, and she gladly accepted it.

"He talk too fast. I can't hear it. But he don't like him," Leena continued.

"What else do you know, Leena?" Cindy urged. She squeezed Kofi's hand.

"He say you right about the money. He knew. He don't trust her."

Cindy's eyes flew to Kofi.

"Tremaine?" Cindy whispered.

Leena nodded.

"What else do you know, Leena?" Cindy asked again.

"Gus a good cat. He know too," Leena added.

Now that Kofi was over the shock that they were basically with two beautiful psychics, he could see a bit more clearly.

"Gus hissed at Stasia," Kofi offered.

Cindy gasped. "That wasn't the first time either."

"Leena, is Cindy in danger? Does she need to get out of that house?" Kofi asked.

Leena shook her head. "She got Celina and Alonzo. And Dorothy, Bernice, and Cissy."

Cindy whimpered. "Those are my grandmothers and my great aunt."

Kofi sighed. It was a relief to hear she had protection, even if it was in the spirit realm.

"Cindy got they grandparents and they parents too. She might be scared, but she is safe. They all here. They nice, but they don't play. Huh, Mama?" Leena said with a huge smile on her face.

Kofi watched tears fall from Cindy's face. "My ancestors are with me?"

"Yes, they are," Halle added. "And Leena is right; they don't play about you. They made it clear when you arrived."

"What do I do now?" Cindy asked. She released Kofi's hand and pulled out a small notebook to write down the child's words.

"Kooohfeee," she stressed as if she wanted to ensure she got it right. "Supposed to take yo' sister with a S to a sneaker dance."

"What?" Kofi shrieked. He was fine to be with Cindy to serve as her emotional support, but he didn't want shit to do with her shady relatives.

"If she think he like her like he like you, Cindy, she gon' tell everything that happened."

Cindy sighed in relief. "Thank you, Leena," she crooned. Cindy lifted and joined Leena on the floor. "It means so much to me."

"You believe me now?" Leena asked and looked up for the first time since she started coloring.

Cindy nodded.

"This for you and Koofee," Leena said as she handed her the picture she worked on.

It was an elementary rendering of a picture of Cindy, Alonzo, and Kofi from his wedding. They took that picture in February, and Kofi had a printed copy. There were blue blobs throughout the background of the picture amongst three bright red ones.

"What's this?" Kofi asked. He pointed at the red spots.

"The bad part around your family. The T, S, and L," Leena responded.

Tremaine, Stasia, and Landry.

Leena stood and accepted Cindy's hug. "You gon' be safe. But you might get scared. Them red parts real, but there's too many blues. They don't win, 'cause the blue is your strong ancestor family."

Cindy blew out a breath and smiled. Kofi stood and helped Cindy to her feet.

"Do you want to know your future together?" Halle asked. Her expression softened as she studied them.

Kofi's heart fluttered. He'd wanted Cindy since he met her in college. If there was a chance he could hear how it turned out for them in the future, he was all for it.

"No. We'll let whatever this is unfold organically," Cindy responded with a blush.

"At least let me ask how many kids we're gonna have," Kofi teased. He could respect her decision. Besides, it wasn't a question of if with them, but when. She'd need the space to avenge and grieve her father's death. He wasn't sure if she was up for a relationship at that point. He would be patient because she was worth it.

"Thank you for having us," Cindy said as they walked to the door.

"Not a problem. Please let us know if we can be of service in the future," Halle said with Leena at her side.

As they reached the door, Leena walked up to Kofi and tugged on his pants. She motioned for him to bend down. Afraid of what might happen if he didn't, he complied.

With her little hand cuffed around his ear, she whispered, "Four."

Kofi swallowed. His eyes were wide, and he hadn't blinked. Leena, on the other hand, giggled.

Chapter Nine

Kofi went through the motions at work. It was late September, and he was grateful for the interns because training them filled his days. His mind stayed on Cindy. Although he was confident in Leena's declaration that she was safe, he still didn't like that she was in the house with at least two untrustworthy people. How were they treating her? And how would they be exposed?

Cindy asked if they could get together over the weekend to discuss Leena's suggestions. She wanted to plan and welcomed Kofi's support. The last thing he needed was for Cindy to go rogue and go at any of this alone.

Kofi: Let's talk at my place

Cindy: okay. You ready for me to meet your family?

Kofi: Hell, no! But we can't talk at your house

Cindy: That's fine

Kofi: How's it going over there?

Cindy: The same. But Dreeyah hugged me today

Kofi: Willingly?

Cindy: LOL, yeah. Leena was right about her. She walked off when I saw her crying

Kofi: monotone, I'll cut you, Dreeyah?

Cindy: I know right. Shouldn't you be working?

Kofi: Working is for interns. When you gonna be my intern again?

Cindy: I requested to start in January. Hopefully I'll be in a better space by then

Kofi: I hope so too. I'll pick you up at six

Cindy: Heart eyes emoji

Kofi left work an hour later, too excited to stick around. No one batted an eye. He was convinced he'd be forced to clock in and out since he was new, but he quickly learned that if the hospital had coverage and he carried his weight with patients, he could come and go as he pleased. He drove home and rehearsed the conversation he wanted to have with his family about Cindy.

His father would be reasonable, but he couldn't say the same for his mother and his brothers. He'd only brought a girl home once, and he hadn't intended for her to meet anybody. The family was supposed to be at one of Maurice's flag football games that was canceled at the last minute due to weather. This would be completely different. He liked Cindy a lot.

His mom would pick up on it. His brothers would be nosy and embarrassing. *Fuck!* He asked his virtual assistant to call his cousin.

"Calling Felicia," the robotic voice declared.

"Hey, Kofi. Where you been?"

"It's a long story."

"David has been a wreck," she said of Alonzo's brother.

"David? You're still seeing him?"

"Don't sound so surprised," Felicia said.

"It's not like you've dated anybody for more than a week."

"It's not serious, but I liked his brother. He seemed nice. How's the princess?"

"It's way too much to get into now. Can you stop by around six?"

"Why? What's up?"

"She's coming over and I need—"

"A buffer?" Felicia joked.

"Yes."

"I got you. Can I bring David?"

"Huh?"

Felicia burst into laughter. "He's not that old, and he's with me now. We'll be there."

"Thank you."

He disconnected the call as he parked his car in the driveway. Detective Landry's car was in front of his parents' home. He hustled to the front door and burst in.

"Here's Kofi now," his mother, Norma Carter, sang.

"You got a warrant?" Kofi boomed.

"Kofi!" His mother spat.

Landry stood. "Why would I need a warrant?"

"I don't consent to you being in my house."

"I was just having a conversation with Mrs. Carter," he said. Landry had lost his mind. He couldn't come and go as he pleased on Kofi's watch. This was his got damn house and his mother.

"Mama, what he ask you?"

"He asked about somebody named Cynthia. I told him we don't know anyone by that name," she responded. Her eyes bounced between her youngest son and the detective.

"I was just about finished. I have one last question?" Landry continued.

"Sure—"

"We exercise our right to remain silent."

"Kofi," his mother urged.

"No, Mama. We exercise our right to remain silent. And unless you have a warrant, I need you to step outside my house."

Landry stood silent for several moments before he shifted his gaze from Kofi's mother then back to him.

"Have yourself a good evening, ma'am," Detective Landry said to Norma as he headed for the door and left.

"Boy, what has gotten into you?"

Kofi held up his hand to tell her to wait until the man was gone.

"I know you done lost your mind," she said as she stood and slapped his hand away.

"I'm sorry. I don't trust him."

"You know him?"

"Yes. Where's Dad? You were in here with him alone?" Kofi asked with his eyes all over the place. The nerve of Landry to come to his house. It had to be to intimidate him. *Did he say I had something to do with Alonzo's death? Was he trying to frame me? Shit!*

"They're out in the field. Kofi, who is Cindy Ella?"

"That's what I came home to tell you." Kofi pulled a chair out to sit, then froze.

"What is it?" she asked, her eyes full of concern.

"Did he call her Cindy Ella?" Kofi's blood cooled.

The ever-present chill he'd gotten since Cindy confided in him about Alonzo's death ran the length of his spine. Mama Tremaine was the only person who called Cindy by that name. Had Detective Landry already spoken to Tremaine without Cindy's knowledge? Was that why she acted suspicious when he spoke to Cindy?

"Detective Landry said he was investigating the death of a young girl's father. The girl's name is Cindy Ella and her father, Alonzo Miller."

Kofi plopped into the chair and rubbed the side of his temple. This wasn't how he wanted to introduce his mom to the future mother of his four children. He chuckled to himself. He was over the moon about Leena's revelation concerning their children.

"What's going on?" his mother quizzed. "Do you know what happened? Please, God, tell me you didn't have anything to do with this."

Kofi was deeply introspective when her words registered. "He said I was involved?" He shrieked.

"Calm down. The detective hinted that she wouldn't have been able to pull it off by herself. Maybe I've watched too many crime shows, but he asked about you and if you'd been in trouble. Anyone would have walked away from the conversation thinking he was trying to build a case against you and Cindy Ella," his mother said. She was still seated, but her eyes were on the table as she mindlessly straightened it.

"Cindy."

"What?"

"Her name is Cindy. And she literally wouldn't hurt a fly."

"Why am I just now hearing about her, Kofi?"

"I... It's complicated, Ma," he said with his shoulders slumped.

"Talk to me, son. I'm listening."

He bounced his knee. Why was it so hard for him to tell her the truth?

"Remember I tried to tell you about Jason's slumber party?"

"The day you and your brothers had that awful falling out?"

"Yes, ma'am. I saw a woman getting assaulted," he admitted.

His mother clutched her chest but said nothing.

"I went to get help, but I should have waited for details about her or the aggressor—"

"Kofi, you were twelve."

"I know, Mama. But you asked why I haven't mentioned Cindy."

"What does she have to do with this?"

He craned his head upward and prayed he could make her understand.

"By the time I told Jason's parents, and they called the police, the woman was gone. I didn't have any details to help her. I thought I was supposed to take my time with Cindy, but every time we get close to making it official, something happens."

He was all over the place. It was as though he'd bottled everything up, and it bubbled to the surface all at once.

"We were together the night her father died. I was going to make it official, but when we arrived at her house, her dad had passed. I can't stay quiet this time, Ma. I saw Detective Landry at the club the night I was with Felicia and Cindy. He was there, and maybe with Tremaine."

It dawned on him as he updated his mother that the woman in the club with Landry was Mama Tremaine. She carried herself with an air of royalty that was not only uncommon but rather sexy. He remembered how distracted he was by her beauty the first time he saw her face on a video call with Cindy. Then later at the wedding, he'd keyed in on her walk and how she carried herself. It was why he told Alonzo he was a lucky man.

"Who is Tremaine?" She barely blinked as she hung on to Kofi's every word.

"Cindy's stepmother. Cindy asked me for help. She says her father was killed. And something is off with the detective. Him being here ain't right."

"Take a breath," his mom said as she stood and placed a hand on her youngest child's shoulder. "I'm worried about you. And if what you're saying is true, I'm worried about Cindy too."

"I had every intention of telling you about her tonight because she's coming over."

A smile spread across his mother's plump cheeks. "You like this girl?"

He nodded. "I've never met anybody like her. She's kind, and weird, and fine."

His mother giggled.

"She's an intern at the hospital. Or at least she was supposed to be. She hasn't started because of everything with her dad."

Kofi filled his mother in on the rest of the details about Cindy and her father. How he'd attended the wedding and about the money. He expressed how he didn't like the fact that she still stayed with them, and he was honest about Leena and her suggestion to solve the mystery on their own.

"I don't like this, Kofi. And you want to pull Felicia into this?"

"She's already involved because of David," he mumbled.

"Who's David?"

"I'm gonna get dressed and go pick up Cindy. I'll let your niece tell you all about David." With a huge smile on his face, he kissed his mother and left her where she stood.

* * *

Kofi's home was cozy. Cindy could fall into a restful sleep for the first time in months. But they had work to do before she would allow herself the luxury.

"Ma, this is Cynthia Miller. Cindy, this is my mother, Norma Carter."

"It's very nice to meet you, Mrs. Carter," Cindy sang. Kofi had his mother's eyes—kind and mysterious. She was like home.

Norma pulled her into a hug. "It's nice to meet you too. I'm so sorry for your loss."

It was frustrating when people hit her with that very popular and well-meaning, yet useless sentiment. But there was immense love wrapped in each of her words when Norma said it. Cindy melted into Norma and allowed the care from her spirit to surround her. She'd been desperate for motherly love, and here it was.

"Thank you," Cindy mumbled with her head resting against her large chest.

"It's okay, dear. Kofi's going to help you figure out what happened. He can do whatever he puts his mind to."

Cindy lifted and swiped the tears from her eyes. "She knows about my dad?"

"Landry was here when I got home from work," Kofi revealed.

"Really?" Cindy asked as her eyes bounced between Norma and Kofi.

Kofi nodded. When she finally separated from Norma's warmth, Kofi led her into their living room. They both took a seat on the extended couch and went silent when Norma joined them.

Cindy prayed she didn't get the wrong impression. She and Kofi had been on the road to being a real couple, but right now her father was her highest priority. Did Norma assume Cindy saw her as a mother-in-law? Mortified, Cindy chewed on the side of her thumb.

"What's the plan?" she asked with a sparkle in her eyes.

Kofi's mother was thrilled to assist in the vindication of Cindy's father. It was cute, and so was she.

"Ma," Kofi groaned.

The two of them stared at each other with identically shaped eyes, until she finally caught the hint.

"Oh, right." She giggled. "I'll leave the two of you to it." As she shuffled her heavy body toward the doorframe, she added, "Please be careful."

"We will, Mom," was Kofi's response.

Cindy grasped her throbbing head. She had a terrible headache. Landry had come to Kofi's home. For what?

"You okay?" Kofi asked once they were alone. "That was a dumb question. How can I help?"

"You already are. And it's not a dumb question. I'm ready to figure out what happened, and I'm afraid I might do something irrational because I'm tired of waiting. Somebody in my house knows who killed my dad."

Kofi filled Cindy in on what happened when he got home and found Landry was there. Along with her throbbing head, her stomach did somersaults. Landry had access to their homes and now Kofi's loved ones. There was no telling what he was capable of.

"Give me your foot."

She regarded him for several moments before she relented. He removed her sneaker and pulled her foot in his lap. Kofi's nimble fingers rubbed and kneaded her foot like it was his second profession.

"Leena said I was supposed to take Stasia to a sneaker dance. Have you heard about one in the area?"

Cindy nodded. She did everything in her power to hold back her moan. Kofi was a gifted man in many ways. His hands squeezed the sole of her foot while his thumb pressed away any remaining stress she had left.

"Can you check online and see where it is?"

Cindy unlocked her phone and went to her social media. Within minutes, she saw a flier for a Winter Sneaker Ball. She was so relaxed at that point that in lieu of words, she simply aimed the phone in his direction.

The students and alumni of the local Gullah and Geechee colleges are hosting their first Winter Sneaker Ball on October 1st. Attire is formal but pull out your best sneakers for footwear. Princes, bring your princess to an event neither of you will forget.

"Do you know how much I love sneakers?"

"I noticed you rarely wear the same pair twice," he observed.

"I'm kind of salty you'll be there with Stasia," she admitted.

"Is that so? I'll be sure to send you pics."

She snatched her foot and pushed him in the chest.

"Look, I'm trying to lighten the mood. I don't want shit to do with her, especially if she was involved with what happened to Alonzo."

A hush fell between them. Kofi reached down and grabbed her other foot, removing her other sneaker when he did.

"How is this going to work? What if she doesn't want to go with me?"

Cindy laughed sarcastically. "Stasia won't need much convincing, especially if she thinks I want you. That's probably your way in."

"What?"

"When you hit her up, pretend like you're talking to us both."

"Yikes."

"I know. Hit her with the 'what you doing' text on instabook, then work your magic until she agrees to go to the ball with you."

Kofi's shoulders sank.

"Take one for the team," she teased.

"Should we find another detective? I almost think I need a wire or something. How are we going to prove anything she tells me?"

Cindy considered his words. She agreed they needed help, but after Landry revealed himself to be involved, she wasn't sure who they could trust.

"I wouldn't want him to find out. Aren't they like a crazy brotherhood? If we went to someone else, who's to know if they wouldn't tell Landry everything we found out, just for him to sabotage our efforts?"

Kofi opened his mouth to speak when two smaller, but equally handsome versions of him bounded through the door.

"What the hell we got here?" the older of the bunch asked as his eyes locked on Kofi's hands on Cindy's feet.

She wiggled out of his grasp and hopped up. "You must be Kofi's oldest brother, Maurice," she said and pulled him in for a hug. "It's nice to finally meet you." She shifted her attention to his middle brother. "And you have to be Devin, right?"

Devin nodded and practically drooled on himself. She grabbed his face between her hands and said, "You are too handsome for your own good. I see where Kofi gets it."

She laid it on thick, but she was acutely aware of the dissension between Kofi and his brothers. If she learned anything from her father's unexpected passing it was that nobody had forever. It was time for them to let go of their two against one dynamic—no matter how different they were.

"You got any sisters?" Maurice asked.

They were dirty from their time outdoors, but in a charming, hardworking way.

"Yes," she admitted, but only one of them was worth it.

"Cindy—" Kofi started.

But Cindy did have someone in mind for him. "You would be a great match for a coworker of Kofi's. Her name is Ava."

Kofi chuckled.

"Right?" she asked as she winked in his direction.

"She ugly?" Maurice asked, offended.

Although they were the older of the Carter boys, Kofi was clearly the most mature.

"She has an ass you can see from the front," Cindy whispered.

"What about me?" Devin interjected.

Cindy held up her phone and showed him a picture of her with one of her sisters.

"Who is that?" he squealed.

"Damn, she's fine, but she looks like she's mean as hell," Maurice added.

"Must be Dreeyah," Kofi added with a laugh.

Cindy nodded.

"I like a challenge," Devin responded, smiling. His smile was twin to his younger brother, Kofi, only without the chipped tooth. He would melt Dreeyah's resolve the same way her father had. Her shoulders sagged at the memory. She gazed down at her cellphone and decided to check on her.

Cindy: Hey, sis. How are you holding up?

Dreeyah: crying tears emoji I'm a mess. I've never cried so much in my life. I'm also a flaming bitch. I should be asking how you are? You upstairs?

Cindy: I'm out. Needed some air. And it's okay. I know you don't do touchy feely.

Dreeyah: It's like we're the only ones who miss him

"Okay, cool. You can stay." Maurice gushed. "Good job, bro."

The brothers slapped hands, and Cindy didn't miss the shocked expression on Kofi's chocolate face.

"Damn, girl. You're a magician. They haven't spoken to me in a long ass time."

Cindy forced a smile. "You mean a princess."

Kofi sat next to her on the sofa. "What happened?"

She showed him the texts from Dreeyah.

"Leena's the magician. She said Dreeyah loved him."

Cindy swallowed the lump in her throat and swiped the tear from her eye. "Text Stasia."

Kofi sucked in a breath and retrieved his phone from his back pocket. He found her profile and texted her. Within seconds she responded.

Stasia: Hey yourself

Kofi: Didn't want to like your pics, but they're fire

Stasia: I knew you liked me. I won't tell

He held the screen so Cindy could see the entire exchange. The hair on her arms stood. She could have been a shady wench, or maybe she was simply unbothered that Kofi was involved with her stepsister. Either way, Stasia's quick response didn't sit right with Cindy. She nodded her head toward the screen to urge him on. Kofi was uncomfortable with his assignment, but Leena claimed this was how they would find out their unanswered questions about her dad.

Kofi: I like that

Stasia: What took you so long?

Kofi sighed, but Cindy elbowed him. "Please."

The desire she saw in Kofi's eyes brought a different type of chill across her sensitive skin. *It's hard to focus when he's this damn fine. It's like he wants me to seduce him.* When he pulled his bottom lip between his teeth, she got a peek at that chipped tooth that turned her on. Maybe it was his pretend flirting with Stasia, but her body wanted him in whatever way she could have him given the circumstances. One moment, she was full of fury over her father's likely murder; the next, she toyed with Kofi, and in the very next breath, she wanted them to progress past friendship.

Cindy leaned over and kissed his earlobe. His eyes drifted closed. When they opened, the desire in them practically reached out and undressed her. He refocused on his phone and continued.

Kofi: Your sister

Anger, sadness, betrayal, and the sense of a loss of control over her future manifested itself in the seductress she was convinced Kofi wanted. She leaned over and shoved her tongue in his ear. He moaned. His eyes darted around the living room toward the door and back to his phone.

Stasia: What she don't know won't hurt her

Kofi: That's how you feel?

Cindy moved her efforts from his ear to his neck and sucked. Kofi concealed a growl that rumbled deep in his throat.

Stasia: 871-555-6982

As Kofi programmed Stasia's number into his phone, Cindy mounted his lap, turned on by the sight of him in his scrubs and his flirting with her shady stepsister. She moved her head to his other ear.

"I'm trying to text your sister," he taunted.

She clamped down on his neck, and he cried out in pleasure.

"You want me to stop?"

He reared his head back to face her. "Are you serious? The only reason I haven't taken you to my room is because I don't wanna disrespect you with my family here."

"I don't care about that," Cindy admitted.

Kofi stood, and Cindy wrapped her legs around his waist. "Damn, girl. I'mma try my best not to scream," he teased.

"It won't bother me one bit."

He kissed her and squeezed her ass where they stood.

"Shit!" She cried. His hands were a heavenly torture. It was about time he relieved the pressure between her legs. "I need this," she confessed.

He pulled back from her and started toward his room.

"Well, hello," his father Samuel boomed.

"Fuck," Kofi muttered.

Cindy wiggled out of Kofi's arms and smoothed her clothes. She must have looked like a thirsty thot in his son's arms. They were in a shared space in the home, and he had no idea who she was.

"I'm Cindy," Cindy said as she extended her hand.

"I'm Kofi's dad. You can call me Sammie." There was a twinkle in his eyes as he regarded her. "How you know Kofi?" Sammie asked.

"I met Kofi when I was at Gullah, and he was a student at Geechee. We kind of lost touch until about a year ago."

"Is that right? Kofi's mother went to Gullah." Sammie gushed. "Who are your folks?"

A sadness washed over Cindy at the reminder that she didn't have any. How could she keep letting herself get distracted? Kofi had become a distraction to where her head should be. She couldn't properly grieve and release her dad until she found out how he was taken from her.

"Celina and Alonzo Miller. They're both dead."

Cindy's gaze was on the hardwood floor until she was tugged in Sammie's direction. "I'm sorry. I didn't know. You're welcome here anytime."

Kofi sighed. "Thanks, Dad."

His hugs were almost as comforting as his wife's. When he loosened his grip, she swiped her eyes.

"Anytime, Cindy. You're welcome here," Sammie repeated after he pulled his son in for a quick hug. "I'll leave the two of you to it. You have a bedroom with a door, son," his father said as he left the living room.

"You can't catch a break," Cindy said to Kofi, joking. Her smile didn't reach her eyes.

"I'm a patient man," he offered. "I'm more concerned about you and what you need."

The fire that he lit when he messaged Stasia threatened to return but was once again interrupted when Felicia and Uncle David burst through the living room door.

Chapter Ten

Felicia and Cindy's uncle agreed to help in any way they could. They were both speechless when Cindy filled them in. Kofi backed up her claims about Leena and swore she hadn't made any of it up. They all decided not to involve the police since they couldn't be sure who they could trust. Between Felicia's loyalty to Kofi and David's commitment to his late brother, they were fully onboard.

Cindy pushed Kofi to text Stasia almost daily. It got to the point that Kofi loathed his text alerts. If it wasn't Cindy, he didn't want to engage. His body ached for her, but he'd also grown tired of her back and forth with him. It had been a year of that, and he deserved more. He would put his sexual urges and desire to be her man aside for now. She'd lost her father, and avenging him would be their focus. After that, if she was on some just friend bull, he was done.

Stasia: I'm nervous about the ball

Kofi: Who is this? Sexy Stasia ain't scared of shit

He ran his hand across his smooth head as he awaited her text. They'd been at it for two weeks nonstop. The dance was this Saturday, and his lunch break had been interrupted by her message.

Stasia: Cindy's going to find out when you pick me up

Kofi: Who said I was picking you up

Stasia: You would pick her up

Kofi. That's different. You ain't no princess. That's why I fuck with you. I can be myself with you.

*Stasia: I should be offended, but you're right. I don't need a fairy-tale. Just a fine ass chocolate man with a big *eggplant emoji*

Kofi: How you know it's big?

Stasia: I can tell by the way you walk. Tell me I'm wrong

This should be Cindy. They should be the ones flirting. She'd been busy with plans for the coming weekend. Cindy and Felicia had grown close. They'd been on a three-way call with his mother last night when he got home. It was his mother's idea to have him wear surveillance equipment hidden in a button on his jacket. They had even provided him with prompts to get her to spill her guts during the dance.

Kofi: Hey

Cindy: Shouldn't you be working and flirting with my sister

Kofi: Not funny. And I'm doing both. I'd rather be flirting with you

Cindy: I don't know what to say

Kofi: Never mind

At the same time, Stasia's texts came through in a cluster.

Stasia: Sis don't appreciate you like I can

Stasia: She probably done gave you blue balls by now

Stasia: Imma suck your dick through your pants

Kofi: Huh?

Sweat beaded on his brow. Strippers did shit like that in the club. Stasia was a freak. Her timing was spot on. Kofi was at war with his mind's preoccupation with how she was likely involved in a cover up and how little his dick gave a damn. He hadn't fucked anyone since he fooled around with Cindy at homecoming. He did have blue balls, and the cold showers had long ago stopped working.

Stasia: I won't be able to wait for us to be alone. The moment we are, I'm sucking your dick through your pants. You might need a change of clothes after, cause it's gonna be messy.

"Shit!" Kofi said aloud.

"Is that Cindy?" Ava asked.

When did she get in here?

"Nah... I mean, yeah."

"Okay, weirdo. I wanted you to tell her thanks for setting me up with Maurice. I haven't met him in person yet, but we've done video chats." She gushed.

He was happy for her and his brother. Maurice hadn't mentioned speaking to Ava, but he was hyped for them anyway. Ava was the type of woman who would have Maurice's life cleaned up in no time. He would get a job and happily spend everything he earned on her. Luckily for him, Ava wouldn't take advantage.

"That's cool."

"Yeah, it is. I'm about to go have lunch with him in my car."

He wrinkled his brows and looked toward the door.

She lifted her lunch bag and phone. "Online still. But soon," she said with crossed fingers. Ava waved and left the break room. The distraction helped to calm his confused libido.

Cindy: I don't know what to say because we keep getting interrupted. I've been hot and cold with you, but every time I'm hot, somebody or something comes up. It's not on purpose I swear.

Kofi understood but powered his phone down. What he needed more than anything was a break from the Miller sisters.

* * *

The Winter Sneaker Ball was tonight, and Cindy was a wreck. Her stomach was in knots, and she couldn't keep still. This was the day she would finally get answers. Because of the way she met Leena, she had faith in her instructions for Kofi to take Stasia to the dance. His patience was thin with her, yet he continued to build a rapport with Stasia to earn her trust.

They hadn't spoken in a couple days. She'd asked too much of him. He wanted to be with her, and she'd driven him into the hands of an alleged accomplice to her father's murder. Times like these, she wished she had a mother. What should she do?

Was it wrong to ask Kofi to put his feelings aside for her? She dialed her fairy godmother.

"Cynthia, how are you, dear?" She hummed.

"Not good."

"Are you safe?"

She and Kofi made it a habit to ask if she was safe whenever they conversed. They wanted to know if anyone else would hear them if she spoke freely.

"I'm on the trail behind my house."

Professor Brenton relaxed. "Good. Tell me what's on your heart."

"I think I want to be with Kofi."

"You think?"

"I know I wish he'd take control. If he leaves it up to me, we'll stay friends."

"Is that what you want?"

Cindy watched as a pair of birds twisted and turned in flight together. They were about to mate, and the sight made her heart flutter. For weeks, she'd lost her connection to the great outdoors. She had to force herself to leave the house. Now, the urge to walk dogs and return to the hospital was back.

"I asked him for help, and he agreed. Part of me wishes he would put his foot down. It hurts him to be near me since we aren't together."

"Let me ask you a question, love."

"Okay."

"Is vulnerability and consent a turn off?"

Cindy laughed nervously. "I wouldn't say it's a turn off."

"Too passive, right? He should whisk you off your feet and demand you be with him?" Professor Brenton continued.

She was gentle in her delivery, and Cindy appreciated her for it.

"Yes."

Professor Brenton chuckled. "That has its place in the bedroom, I agree. But in life, have you ever allowed yourself to be cherished and claimed without all the bravado and disregard for your feelings?"

Cindy respected Professor Brenton, but her man needed to come correct. If not, he belonged in the friend zone.

"Who was the last man who approached you in the way you prefer?"

"Dante."

"Where is Dante now? Has he reached out since your father passed?"

He hadn't. But that was okay. He wasn't her counselor, and they didn't do much talking. They fucked, and she liked it.

"Professor Brenton, this is Kofi now," she lied. "I need to take this."

"Call me anytime. And Cynthia?" she urged.

"Yes?"

"Consider if you'll be okay when Kofi moves on. Because a handsome, caring man like that eventually will."

"Okay."

Cindy disconnected the call. *Would Kofi choose another woman?* It pissed her off when he saw the girl with the stripper shoes in his face at the bar. Maybe she should be sure she could handle it when Kofi tired of her indecision. He hadn't called, but he did send a text.

It was a picture of him in his formal attire. His white dress shirt was fitted with the top few buttons undone. He paired it with blue pants and a pink moth blazer that had a blue handkerchief in the pocket. He was mouthwatering. He'd flashed his chip toothed smile at the camera.

Kofi: How do I look?

Cindy: Good enough to eat

Shit, I'm in trouble.

She walked back home more confused than ever. "Daddy, I miss talking to you," she said aloud. "I don't know where you are, but I hope you hear me. Can you hear me?"

A hummingbird flew in front of Cindy's face. She froze. She'd never been this close. If she lifted her head, she'd bump it with her nose. The bird stayed suspended in air in front of her for a full minute before she accepted it had been sent there by her father.

The hummingbird fluttered away. Relief filled Cindy's body, and Leena's words rang in her head. *"She got Celina and Alonzo. And Dorothy, Bernice, and Cissy."*

It was sunset when she arrived back home. Kofi's car was parked in her driveway. It was showtime. With sweaty palms, Cindy opened the door. There was yelling.

"You got some fucking nerves showing up here. After all Cindy's been through!" Dreeyah yelled at Kofi.

Any question of whether Dreeyah was involved melted from the recesses of Cindy's mind. She was a real one. Dreeyah loved Alonzo just as Leena said.

Stasia was dressed to kill. She stood to the side with a sneer on her face and her fingers intertwined with Kofi's. Her eyes scanned him from his bald head to his fresh kicks.

"Cindy has made it clear that we're nothing more than friends. Ask her yourself." Kofi's tone and cadence were measured.

Cindy flinched at his words. They were acting, right?

"It doesn't matter. We all saw how you were with her at the wedding. Her father's wedding, by the way, asshole. And now you're here to take Stasia out?"

Dreeyah was beside herself. She didn't lose her cool for anyone. The only time she smiled in that house was for Alonzo. She was neither happy nor bothered otherwise.

"That's between you and your twin," he said.

"I'll deal with her treacherous ass later," Dreeyah spat. "Make this make sense, Kofi. You're taking Stasia to a ball? Hell, I can't stand how much of a princess Cindy is, but she's undeniable. And a sneaker ball at that. Stasia doesn't even own sneakers. Those look like Cindy's!"

She moved like she would slap Kofi or Stasia—they stood side by side so Cindy couldn't be sure—but before things got physical, Tremaine entered the room with a deep frown on her face. "What is wrong with you?" she asked Dreeyah and stepped in front of her, holding her arm.

For the first time, Cindy spoke up. "Why are you holding Dreeyah?"

Everyone looked at Cindy who'd silently watched the scene unfold until then.

"She's acting irrationally. You told me yourself that Kofi was a friend, and I let it be known then he was a better catch than Dante."

Kofi's jaw clenched at the mention of Dante. There was no need for him to be bothered. She hadn't spoken to him since summer.

"Why should such a handsome young man go to waste? When Stasia said she was going to go out with Kofi tonight, I thought it was a great idea."

Cindy glared at her. *Adulterous, murdering bitch!* It took every ounce of strength she had not to choke her out. Kofi divulged his suspicions that she'd been with Landry the night they were at the bar. And she was broke. That was motive enough.

Her saving grace was that Cindy wanted to be sure they had proof when they finally went to authorities, especially since she was fucking Landry. Tremaine had him referring to her as Cindy Ella.

"I'm texting Devin," she threatened. "Maybe he can talk some sense into this sad Carter in front of me."

Devin reached out. Good for him. She never doubted that Dreeyah and Kofi's brother were a good match.

"We're gonna be late," Stasia quipped. She leaned up and placed a peck on the corner of Kofi's mouth.

Dreeyah swatted in her twin's direction but was held back by their mother. "I outta kick your ass, Stasia. She don't deserve that."

"Cindy is a big girl. We've all been through hard times. We don't have a dad either." She shrugged her exposed shoulders.

The walls closed in on Cindy. *What did that heffa just say?*

Stasia turned toward the door, foolishly confident she was safe from either of her sisters' hands. Kofi's eyes were locked on Cindy. She couldn't read his expression, and she had to remind herself this was her idea. It was part of the plan. *Kofi still wants me, right?*

"Kofi, let's go, baby," Stasia ordered, and he followed.

* * *

What the fuck am I doing? Kofi stood under the blue light as Stasia backed it up on him. All it did was remind him of homecoming when Cindy had pressed her soft ass against him until he'd had enough and taken her in one of those back rooms. His dick was in hibernation now.

Maybe if Stasia had better character, he could admit she was attractive. But the way she'd spoken to Cindy made his skin crawl. He was tasked with finessing her out of information that would probably land her and her mother in prison.

The look on Cindy's beautiful face while he pretended to be interested in Stasia would forever be burned in his mind's eye. It was the truth when he said Cindy wanted them to be friends. Did she care about something romantic with him after all? Except for Gabrielle, Cindy didn't get jealous. Did she think he wanted Stasia on his arm instead of her? *Hell, no!*

It was her. It was always and only her.

"Let's get a drink. You're not dancing anyway." Stasia heaved.

Kofi peeked at his button for the tenth time. Cindy, Felicia, and David could see and hear everything live. He also had a small device hidden in his ear that they promised only to use to communicate with him if he was backed against a wall. It was another reminder that the woman who had his heart would hear every comment he used on her sister. He prayed she understood he was acting.

They stood at the bar and waited for the bartender.

"That was wild what happened at your house," Kofi offered.

She shrugged. "Cindy's time is up. Ding dong, the king is dead," she teased.

What the fuck? "Who, her dad?"

She nodded. "And now you're here with me. She can finally see what it feels like to be disregarded."

"What you mean by that?" Kofi stepped into her personal space. He brushed a piece of her straight black hair from her face, aware what his proximity would do to her.

Stasia's lips parted. "My dad left and so did hers."

He grabbed the back of her neck and pulled her in like he'd kiss her. Kofi saw the bartender approach. Unlike when he was with Cindy, he was relieved they would be interrupted. "I'm sorry to hear that."

"What can I get you two?" The woman purred, just as Kofi's lips were inches from Stasia's.

Stasia stumped her foot and ordered. Kofi settled for a water he wasn't sure he would drink. Cindy mentioned early on that while she wasn't afraid of living in the house, she said one of her drinks tasted funny. Therefore, she stopped eating anything that wasn't packaged or bottled from inside the house. They took a seat so Stasia could finish her drink. Kofi rested his hand on her thigh and started with one of his prepared prompts.

"You know, Cindy says Alonzo didn't die in his sleep. It's another reason I grew tired of talking to her."

Stasia swung her eyes in his direction but said nothing. He lifted his hand to rest higher on her thigh and traced a circle there.

"Has she always had an active imagination like that?"

"I don't know," she responded on an exhale. "Maybe she thinks that because he didn't."

Kofi's blood cooled at her admission, and three unintelligible voices boomed in his left ear. He leaned into her—with his right side —and whispered, "What did you do, you filthy bitch?" Kofi pressed his lips to the side of her ear the way Cindy had done. The ordeal made his stomach flip. He'd never been this close to a woman with a soft dick. Stasia was nauseating.

She peered up at him with fire in her honey-colored eyes. "I may have put something in a cup of tea."

He wrapped his long fingers around her throat. Her eyes lowered. "What did he do to you?"

"Nothing. I didn't have a problem with Alonzo," she divulged. Her eyes lowered again. And each time she opened them, they were a shade darker.

Kofi tightened his grip on her neck. "Make this shit make sense, Stasia."

"I felt sorry for him," she whispered.

"Why?" Kofi pressed his lips to the side of her ear again, but this time he kissed her.

Stasia moaned and squirmed in her seat. "Because my mother is a cheating whore."

Kofi stilled. "Mama Tremaine loved Alonzo; she didn't cheat. You're lying," he bluffed.

"My mom has never been faithful a day in her life. That's why my dad beat her up. Among other things."

"You a cheater like your mama?" he asked, tightening his grip on her neck.

"I wouldn't cheat on you, I swear."

"Would you lie to me?" Kofi kept on.

She shook her head as much as she could with his fingers wrapped around her neck. The dim blue light and the position of their seats in the back of the ballroom made it difficult for other attendees to see Kofi's risky behavior.

"If you felt sorry for him, why did you give him the shit in the tea?" Kofi asked. He was disgusted but too invested to give up now. Her ass needed to go to prison.

"I made the tea for Cindy. With her out of the picture, he

would've eventually given us everything he had. Grief is a tricky thing."

"Don't lie to me!" Kofi spat. He flattened his tongue and licked the side of her face. She liked kinky shit, and he would do whatever he had to get her full confession.

"I'm not, baby, shit!" Her body vibrated from the contact. "I made the tea for Cindy. He must have gotten it somehow and drank it. At first, I was scared, but my mom's side man is a detective."

"You lying to impress me, Stasia? 'Cause I'm not buyin' it," he pressed.

She squirmed in her seat. "I had the conversation with him at the back of the house near the door in case he tried to flip it on me."

"What the hell does that have to do with anything?" Kofi smoothly pulled her onto his lap and shifted his hand so it was still around her neck.

Cindy's voice bellowed, 'Damn', in his ear. She stayed turned on by him at the most inappropriate times. He'd told Cindy she could have this treatment anytime she wanted. And when he did it with her, he would mean it.

"It's on the video doorbell app. I saved it," she spilled.

"Show me," he demanded.

She craned her neck to see him, and he licked her face again. With shaky fingers, Stasia whipped out her phone and pulled up the app. When she navigated to the video, he stood. She fell from his lap and gasped. Stasia liked to be handled roughly.

"I can't hear shit in here. Show me outside, or you a fucking lie."

She pulled him toward the exit. Once they were outside, she navigated to the video and turned up the volume. Sure enough, Detective Landry was at the back of Cindy's house with Stasia.

The audio was a little fuzzy with interjections from crickets and cicadas. But the two of them were easily identifiable, and their voices were loud enough that the video would transmit through the button on his clothes.

"What was so important that you had to pull me away from your mother?" Landry's shifty ass said on the video. Even on the small screen, Kofi could make out his ginger-colored hair.

"I tried to get rid of his daughter, but he drank the shit you gave me."

Landry rubbed his temples. "Don't panic. I'll move the cup and keep your mother busy. By the time she finds him, it will look like it happened in his sleep."

"Are you sure?" Stasia asked. She shifted her weight from one foot to the other and looked behind her every few seconds.

"Be cool. I'll make sure it doesn't get back to you. Once the life insurance clears, you'll be set for life," Landry promised.

Stasia put the video away and smiled deviously. "You believe me now."

"Hell yeah. I love that shit," he lied. "Something I ate is fucking with me though."

Disappointment crowded her light brown eyes. "You're sweating."

Kofi was overcome with emotions. He hustled to the edge of the sidewalk and stuck his head out to release the contents of his breakfast. Not only was Leena right, but Cindy's gut had also been spot on from the beginning. She didn't deserve this, and neither did Alonzo.

"You did that shit, cousin," Felicia said in his ear.

"Thank you, baby," Cindy chimed in. She cried, and Felicia and David consoled her.

He'd finally done it. Unlike when he was a child, this time when he went for help, he would have all the details necessary to bring justice for the victim.

"Okay, nephew. We calling the police to meet her here. There's a chance Landry might get wind of it, so I need you to stay cool and keep her convinced that you want her with you," David said into the earpiece.

He nodded.

"I'm gon' drive us home. Can you ride share from my house?" Kofi said to Stasia.

"Or I can stay with you until you feel better."

He nodded again. "I'd like that, you crazy bitch." He slapped her on the ass which earned him a giggle. She was tickled, while he needed to vomit again.

Kofi had to pull over twice to empty his stomach. The second time, there was only an acidic taste and his gastric juices that came up. He basically dry heaved until he was calm enough to finish the drive. Everything had to go as planned. He couldn't let Cindy down like he'd let that woman down. His confidence from the sneaker ball faded, and he was once again filled with doubt.

The next five minutes consisted of him gagging and Stasia rubbing his back. He wanted to slap her hand away but resisted. When they pulled into his long driveway, blue and red lights danced across the property. Stasia's head flew in his direction.

"What the fuck did you do?"

"Nothing," he lied. He parked the car and pretended to be unaware of what the commotion was about.

They stepped out of the car, and the closest officer cuffed her while he read her Miranda rights. She glared at him. He had no idea what she was capable of. Was he safe now that he had her arrested? He couldn't worry about that now. He needed to get to Cindy.

As he made his way through the crowd, Landry had also been cuffed and was being put in the back of a police car. Kofi waved, and his stomach finally settled. Cindy ran toward him and jumped in his arms.

"Thank you, Kofi. He can rest now, thanks to you!"

Chapter Eleven

Cindy was in intense grief counseling for three months following her stepsister and her stepmom's boyfriend's arrests. Her life was turned upside down, and she desperately needed stability. Stasia pled guilty and was awaiting sentencing, while Landry pled not guilty and awaited trial.

Dreeyah moved out and was also in counseling. They kept in contact enough for Cindy to check in on her, although at times it was too much for Cindy to associate with her because of her attachment to Tremaine and Stasia. Tremaine moved in with another boyfriend and stood by Stasia's side more than her free, innocent daughter Dreeyah. It didn't surprise Cindy.

She hadn't spoken to Kofi at all. He'd called and texted her that he didn't need anything from her, just to know she was okay. As the weeks slipped by, he stopped reaching out altogether. She regretted how she treated him. Now that she was in a better headspace, and their old home was sold, she was ready to begin her internship.

Cindy lived with her fairy godmother, Professor Brenton, and spoke with her daily about Kofi. She accepted that she missed out on a chance to have something real with him because of her ghosting. He at least deserved a text. It wouldn't have hurt her to tell him she needed time to get her head straight.

Cindy was set to start at Paradise Pet Care Hospital in a week. She owed Kofi the heads up of a conversation before she started. She stood at the entrance of the hospital with Gus in tow. She probably looked like she'd lost her mind. She wore a teal poofy dress that was fitted at the top and loose at the bottom with a pair of sneakers.

It was what she would have worn had she and Kofi been able to attend the sneaker ball and go on a date without the complications of her personal life. Her father was at rest now. She had peace. And when Kofi saw her, she wanted him to see her like this.

"Okay, Gus. Pretend to be sick," she said. Gus blinked at her and turned his head.

"Hey, Cindy," Ava said when she entered. "Are you here for Kofi, or does this cutie need to be seen?" she asked as her eyes bounced between her gown and Gus.

"Kofi."

Ava gave her a reassuring smile. "You look stunning, Cindy. I'll go get him for you."

Cindy took a seat in the empty waiting room. Fifteen painful minutes later, Ava returned alone. The smile on her face was strained.

"This is awkward," she started. "He doesn't want to see you," she whispered, even though they were the only two in the waiting room.

"Oh, okay. Thank you for asking."

Cindy stood and moseyed toward the door, but she couldn't bring herself to leave.

"Is everything alright?" Ava was behind the counter, her voice full of concern.

Cindy whipped around. "I'm not leaving."

"Huh?"

"Tell Kofi or don't. But I'm not leaving until I see him," Cindy said and took a seat.

"Okay, girl." Ava twittered. She disappeared to the back in fits of small giggles.

He'd been patient with her, so she'd be patient with him. She let Gus explore the cat furniture in the waiting room. A half hour later, he still hadn't come to see her. A little girl with a wet face and a bird cupped securely in her hand entered the office.

"You're so pretty," the young girl said.

"Thank you."

Her mother regarded Cindy curiously.

"I'm waiting for a friend," Cindy offered to the little girl's guardian. The woman gave Cindy one last once over and stood at the counter to check in.

"Can I see?" Cindy asked. She moved from her chair to the floor, unbothered that her gown was on the floor. She was a princess who loved animals and sneakers. A little dirt wouldn't hurt.

The girl nodded. "Her name is Tweet, and I'm Cindy." Her brown cheeks were flushed.

"Can I tell you a secret?"

This time when little Cindy nodded, her eyes lit up.

"My name is Cindy too. And I'm a vet."

"You're a princess *and* a vet?"

"Yes."

Cindy looked at the bird who had a swollen abdomen. When she handed Tweet back to little Cindy, she said, "You'll have to wait until you and your mommy go back with a doctor on duty, but you'll be excited about this belly."

Little Cindy's eyes widened. "Why?"

Cindy whispered, "She's about to lay an egg."

Johns opened the door and sighed. "Again, Miller?"

She smiled at him from the floor and waved to little Cindy. As she and her mother headed to the back, Cindy announced, "I start next week, Dr. Johns."

He huffed again, then closed the door behind him. It had been over an hour, and there was no sign of Kofi. Cindy had no idea what was wrong with the next patient, until the owner said the pig was afraid because the last time they were there, it got vaccinations. The squealing and grunts grew louder. The owner was also nervous, so Cindy did what she knew best: She sang.

"No matter how your heart is grieving, if you keep on believing..."

The pig was quiet, but Cindy stopped when the door flew open. A very handsome and angry Kofi stood and stared at her. She petted the pig one last time and lifted from the floor. His eyes smoldered as they raked over her body appreciatively. She pulled up her dress to show off her sneakers.

"Can I come back now?" she asked.

Kofi's dark chocolate complexion against his baby blue scrubs made her mouth water. "Johns said you were here taking patient histories," he said through gritted teeth.

"All I did was sing this time. AbraHam just doesn't want vaccinations."

"Who?" Kofi stifled a chuckle.

"AbraHam," she repeated.

He nodded his head toward the back and stepped aside for her to enter. She relaxed. It only took him two hours. Kofi was worth it.

$$* * *$$

He led her to a conference room at the far end of the hospital away from the other staff and patients, then slammed the door behind them. She jumped when he did. Once again, Kofi was turned on, despite the tension between them. Where the hell had she been all this time? Did she expect him to drop everything?

Then she had the nerve to look like an actual princess. Cynthia Miller was the most beautiful woman he'd ever seen. She'd done her hair and makeup like they had formal dinner plans. The sneakers were perfect. *She* should have been his date to the Winter Ball. While he was glad to help with Stasia's and Landry's arrests, he could no longer be Cindy's friend whenever she needed him. He drew a line in the sand.

"I'm sorry," she said weakly.

His jaw clenched. He still had an electronic notepad in his hands.

"Does that door lock?" she asked.

He shuddered, and he couldn't force his body not to respond to her. He dropped his hands in front of his manhood. She inched closer to him. Once she was close enough to lean forward and kiss him, she reached around him and locked the door herself. *Shit!*

She raised her hand and rested it on his unkempt facial hair. With her mouth next to his ear, she asked, "You still want me, Kofi?"

He closed his eyes. How long would he continue to torture himself? They were at his job. Someone could knock on the door at any time. She kissed his earlobe, and he snapped. He dropped his work device then reached down and grabbed her by the thighs. She wrapped her legs around him while her dress danced about.

When his hands connected with bare flesh, he froze.

"I didn't wear any," she said, answering his unspoken question.

He walked her to the extended sectional at the side of the room and laid her there. She pulled her spaghetti straps down, exposing more of her luminous skin.

"You want me, Cindy?"

She nodded.

"Just my body?"

She shook her head.

Right answer.

Kofi pushed her dress up—her sexy ass purposely hadn't worn any underwear—and placed his face between her thighs. He'd wanted to do that again since the first time he had the pleasure of sampling her at homecoming. She tasted like honey, and he was hooked after one swipe of his tongue. Cindy's moans tickled his ears. Kofi would savor every moment with her. He didn't give a damn about where they were.

He pulled her bud into his mouth and sucked. He licked then flicked the back of his tongue out at her like an oral spanking. She squirmed, and her thighs clamped against his head. They were so soft he didn't care how tightly she gripped him. Her hands on his head were proof he wasn't in another life-like dream. She was here, and his mouth was on her.

She writhed in ecstasy. All the anger and frustration he had toward her for not calling him dwindled the moment her voice rang out when she sang to an animal in the waiting area. Then he saw her. Although he had been furious that she hadn't bothered to check in, he was hard instantly.

Cindy's moans were louder. He placed two of his fingers inside of her as he worked his tongue between her sensitive folds. By the time he was done, she wouldn't think twice about another man.

"This my pussy, got dammit! You hear me?" he asked between slurps.

Cindy nodded with urgency. "I'm cumming, Koooooooofi," she sang.

Her body quaked, and his member bounced. It was his dick's turn, and it couldn't wait another second. Unbothered by his dick's thoughts, and Cindy's quick movement to remove her dress fully, Kofi stared down at her.

"Marry me," Kofi moaned.

She stilled.

"What?" she asked on an exhale.

"You heard me."

She lifted to her elbows and watched as he stepped out of his scrub pants and stroked his manhood.

"What kind of fourplay game is this?"

"Do I look like I'm playing?"

"Show me the ring," she countered with a smirk on her sexy face.

He reached in the pocket of his scrubs and produced an engagement ring. No box, just the solitary pearl cut diamond fit for his princess.

Her eyes widened. "How long have you had that on you?"

"Since the day after homecoming."

Her eyes closed, and she threw her head back. He removed a condom from his wallet and sheathed himself.

"You gonna take my last name, Cindy?"

"Cynthia Carter?" she moaned.

"Cynthia Miller Carter," he amended.

Tears sprang to her eyes, and he couldn't tell if it was related to thoughts of her father or pure enjoyment. If she agreed, he would love the sadness from her spirit.

"Is that a yes?"

She nodded and held out her hand. He slipped the ring on her finger, and his dick bounced again. Kofi hovered over Cindy, kissing her as he entered her fiercely. She cried out.

"Dr. Carter," she moaned.

He used his thumbs to caress her nipples with the same dexterity required for his video games. It brought a smile to his face to see the passion spread across hers. Her fuck faces made his balls tingle. Convinced he had enough of her tortured expressions, he lowered his head to her titties and pulled a nipple between his teeth. She bucked and arched closer to him.

"You like that?"

Her mouth was opened, but no sound came out. Kofi had waited over a year to be inside of her, and now that he finally was, he was determined to spend all night in it. A small knock sounded at the door, and Kofi stopped his movement. He pulled out and punched the sofa when he did.

"Fuck!" Kofi rasped.

Cindy turned and got on all fours. She wiggled her ass in front of him to urge him on. He was behind her in no time.

"It's Ava," she said from the door. "I heard y'all from the hall-way," she whispered.

"Cover for us, girl!" Cindy wailed.

Ava snickered and scurried away just as Kofi reentered Cindy like a savage. He almost came undone when she continued her fluid movements in front of him. He steadied her with his hands securely on her hips to catch his breath.

"I need it, Kofi. Please."

His eyes rolled to the back of his head. This was his fiancée, the future mother of their four children, and she begged for his dick. What kind of man would he be if he deprived her of it?

He slammed into her, then slowed down to deliver measured strokes. Just when she'd start to squirm, he would slam into her again. This time, he reached in front of her and played with her clit.

"Damn, you so wet."

Cindy hummed. She leaned up and grabbed the back of his bald head, bringing his face down to hers. He rocked in and out of her from the back while their lips tangled in torrid pleasure.

"It's so hard," was Cindy's response.

"You got me like this."

She smirked against his lips.

"Why you make me wait so long?"

"I'm sorry. I can make it up to you."

Kofi's knees buckled, and once again, he was close to his release. "Show me," he demanded.

She slipped out of his grasp before he could respond. Cindy stood before him completely naked.

"Got damn, baby." Her body was unbelievable. Her hips, her titties, and her soft tummy made his mouth water. The best part was that his ring rested on her finger.

She dropped to her knees in front of him and swiped the condom from his dick.

"Baby—"

"We don't need it. You're going to finish in my mouth."

Kofi's toes curled and she hadn't even put her mouth on him yet.

"Is that okay with you?" She breathed against the bouncing beast between his legs.

"Hell yeah."

Cindy wrapped her hot mouth around him. She licked and she sucked.

"Slow down, baby, shit," he tried.

But Cindy had a mind of her own. When she reached between his slightly opened legs and caressed his balls, he squeezed his eyes shut.

"Move, Cindy. I'm about to bust."

She stroked his dick and kept sucking. With her other hand, she continued to massage his balls. When he finally shot his load down her pretty mouth, he almost blacked out. Cindy kept a sexy eye contact with him that had his body shuddering. Then she dramatically swallowed while he watched.

"I think I love you," he whimpered.

She lifted from her knees and mounted him. Beside his ear, she said, "I know I love you."

Chapter Twelve

Cindy twerked around her new apartment as she hummed and cleaned. It was time for her to move out from her fairy godmother's place. Initially she needed the cocoon-like environment as she navigated her way through counseling, but now she was engaged. Each time she got a glimpse of the ring on her finger her heart smiled.

It was easier for Cindy to see pictures of her father. There were only four portraits on the wall so far. One was of Cindy and Alonzo when she was little. It was next to a professional photo of the two of them dancing on the carpet before his wedding to Tremaine. The last two pictures were of Alonzo, Cindy, and Kofi at the wedding. One was taken by the photographer while the other was the sketch Leena colored with the blue ancestors.

"You need help with that, baby?" Kofi asked, startling her. "Did I scare you?" She nodded. "I'm sorry. I probably should have given you some space or called first, but I still can't believe you gave me a key. I'm shocked your ass said yes to my proposal."

"You and me both," she teased.

He used his long arms and pulled her snugly against him. "Am I moving too fast?"

"Yeah, but I like it."

"Finish this later so I can take you out."

Cindy turned to face him fully. The corners of her mouth lifted in anticipation. "Where are we going?"

"Nope, I'm not telling you," he said as he planted a kiss on her forehead and created distance between them. "Get dressed in something comfortable-nice."

"Kofi, what is comfortable-nice?" She laughed at his choice of words.

"No heels, but no sweats either," Kofi told her as if what he said made perfect sense.

She blushed and wet her lips.

He tugged at her waist until she was flush against him. "You like when I tell you what to do?"

She twirled her red hair and cleared her throat. She did like it. It had taken way too long for her to accept her true feelings for Kofi Carter, but now more than ever she wanted him exactly as he was. As if he sensed the introspective shift in her demeanor, he walked her to the nearest chair and sat pulling her onto his lap.

"What's up?"

"Thank you."

"For what?" Kofi wore the biggest grin as he awaited her response. He was absolutely smitten with her and had been from the beginning. Her heart melted at his signature chip-toothed smile.

"For being patient with me. I've been hot and cold with you, and you didn't deserve that."

His smile faded. He was quiet for so long Cindy worried she'd unnecessarily ruined their light-hearted mood.

"You were flighty as hell. All that singing to birds had you acting like them. I should call you Birdie Cindy," he teased. She swatted his arm. "It was worth it. You were worth it, baby."

Cindy leaned in and kissed her fiancé. Her heart picked up a beat at the realization that they were finally together.

"I said I wanted to take you out," he whined between her kisses that grew hotter by the minute.

She turned to straddle him so they were face to face. Her lips found Kofi's neck and his eyes closed. He found her ass and squeezed it. It was a struggle for him to keep his hands off her.

"We have to leave in an hour," he moaned.

"That's plenty of time."

"No, it's not and you know it." He lifted her with little effort and adjusted himself while she watched.

Instead of letting it go, she stood in front of him and pulled her thin shirt over her head.

"What you doin', baby?" Kofi's eyebrows were furrowed like he was in pain.

"I need to shower. I'm dirty from cleaning the apartment."

"Can I come?"

That was her plan all along. She continued to shed clothing and once she was fully naked, she turned toward the bathroom.

"Shit, girl." Kofi undressed despite his insisting they didn't have time.

Cindy belted out a song about love while she twirled her wide hips inside her tiny shower. Her apartment was much smaller than the house where she and her stepfamily lived, but her new space was infused with love in every corner. When Kofi stepped in behind her the change in temperature sent a chill up her spine. Everything on his body was hard including between his legs. She didn't stop her dance, and Kofi stood in a trance just like he'd done at homecoming.

Cindy leaned forward against the wall of the shower and wiggled her backside.

"Bend over, baby," Kofi whined.

Her pulse quickened and she did as she was told. His large hands grasped her hips as she braced herself on wobbly legs. They had sex since he proposed, but her body still hadn't adjusted to his girth.

"Let me in, baby."

Her legs quivered. When he spoke to her like that, she feared she'd lose her damn mind.

"I need it, Cindy. I need it now, baby."

She tooted her ass higher, and Kofi finally slid in.

"Mmhm," she moaned.

"Tell me I can have you," he demanded.

"You can have me, Kofi. I'm yours."

"You mine?" Kofi accented each of his words with forceful thrusts that sent the water in every direction. He used his fingers to reach in front of her and caress her hardened nipples. Her body contorted, and she did her best to grab on to anything to steady herself when the orgasm tore through her. Kofi's hands tightened around her waist as he continued his strokes.

"I love the sounds you make when you cum. I need to see your face."

He withdrew and turned her toward him. With the shower still full blast, he lifted her and backed her against the far end of the wall. Cindy wrapped her shaky legs around the love of her life. The desire in Kofi's eyes sent aftershocks of pleasure coursing through her veins.

"Damn your face is beautiful when I'm inside you," he muttered. He tucked his bottom lip between his teeth.

Cindy's body bucked.

"Cum again, Mrs. Carter," he urged.

Waves upon waves slammed through Cindy. Her eyes rolled upward, and her breathing was disordered. "Yes!"

He leaned closer and pulled her earlobe into his mouth. "You so fucking sexy."

Her eyes found his. There was no way she could handle another orgasm and have the use of her legs for this surprise date. Nothing hurried him along like a profession of her love.

"I love you, Kofi, and nobody else can have me," she said as she stared at him.

"Shit, baby."

"My pussy is all yours," she continued.

Kofi's movements grew chaotic.

"My body and my heart belong to you," she purred.

He thrusted into her one final time and released a throaty growl as he met his peak. "Damn, I love you."

She wrapped her arms around his neck, "I love you too, Dr. Carter."

"Shit!"

She giggled as he released her.

"I almost dropped you, baby."

She did a two-step and reached for the soap. "Now hurry up so you can take me to my surprise."

* * *

When they arrived at their destination, Cindy peered up at Kofi like he hung the stars. The feedback she gave him about their horseback riding date was the fuel for him to step it up a notch. Cindy deserved it.

"Kofi, what did you do?" she asked as he opened her car door.

"I want to show you the world."

Water filled her eyes. "This is the most exciting thing anyone has ever done for me."

He leaned down and kissed the corners of her eyes. There were times she cried seemingly out of nowhere. Kofi was powerless to eliminate her grief, so he'd made it a habit of kissing her tears away. Sometimes she would respond with a faint smile, and he'd give her space while other times it would lead to the two of them making love.

"You scared?" he asked.

"Have you met me?"

To her credit, Kofi had yet to see her flinch at anything dangerous. "Bring your sassy ass on." He turned to leave, but stopped when he didn't feel her by his side. "What?"

She fidgeted and twirled her hair around her finger. He loved the bright red color and the sexy way she dressed up but still wore sneakers. She was turned on by his demands.

He walked back to where she hadn't moved. "Baby, we can do more of that later."

"I'm going to have wet panties the entire ride if you keep talking like that," she admitted.

"Well, shit. Take 'em off," he teased.

The men hustled around them to prepare for a safe experience. Kofi had spent a hefty amount to secure a private hot air balloon ride, but he had a mind to cancel with the energy Cindy gave him and the way she gazed at his mouth.

She reached for his hand. He led her to a safe place to watch as the men inflated the huge balloons. Each time Kofi saw her eyes light up it made every moment of their back-and-forth history together worth it. His heart skipped a beat. He wanted nothing more than to shower Cindy with moments like these until he took his last breath. There was childlike wonder across her beautiful features when the balloons went from laying on the grass to fully erect.

Once they were inside the basket, Kofi, Cindy, and the pilot were lifted from the ground. She hung on to him as she took in the majesty of the trees below them. He felt her eyes on him.

"What's wrong, baby?"

There were tears in her eyes again. He'd gotten better at reading when they were happy or sad tears, but this time he couldn't tell.

"My dad wouldn't have liked me doing this." She chuckled as she spoke with wet cheeks. "But I know he's glad I came to my senses and gave in to you."

Kofi bent down and first kissed her cheeks then her lips. "I'm glad you did too. I can make you happy for the rest of our lives if you let me."

"Okay."

They'd forgotten the pilot was there. He spoke over the radio from time to time, but respectfully blended in the background. Cindy bounced her shoulders and moved from one side of the basket to the next. She peered down at the breathtaking landscape while Kofi watched... her.

"Let me see you."

She stilled, then stole a glance at the pilot. The older gentleman had his face buried in his smart phone. Cindy closed the space between them and split her time between his face and the one-thousand-foot elevation.

"You're missing everything."

Kofi had his back leaned against the side of the balloon. Cindy faced out and he faced her.

"The view is very nice," he said as he slipped his hand down the stretchy fabric of her pants.

"Kofi," she yelped. She peeked over her shoulder once again.

"He ain't worried about us. As much as I paid him, I could pull your pants down and fuck you and he wouldn't say shit."

Her eyes closed and her lips parted. He captured her mouth while his fingers stroked her wet center. She tasted better each time he kissed her, and her panicky moans were a symphony to his ears.

"Kofi," she whined.

He rubbed his pointer and middle finger back and forth creating the friction he needed to please her.

"I already had too many orgasms in the shower, remember?"

He gave her an easy smile while he continued his pleasurable torture. "There's no such thing as too many with me, baby."

"We're now at three-thousand-feet," the pilot announced just as Cindy met her third orgasm of the day.

As her body relaxed and her breathing returned to its natural rhythm, Kofi turned to face the view and pulled Cindy safely under his arm. They watched the clear sky and the top of the trees. This was love.

Chapter Thirteen

Cindy tried unsuccessfully to slip from Kofi's grasp.

"Where you going, baby?" His voice was full of sleep as he wasn't fully awake.

"I need to get ready for work," she whispered, still attempting and failing to lift from the bed.

The sun wasn't up yet, but Cindy wanted to get a jump start to her first day as an intern at Paradise Pet Care Hospital. Kofi was a bit of a morning person, but only after he'd had his coffee. She made a mental note to make him a cup once she was dressed.

He shook his head with his eyes still closed. "It's dark. Come back."

Cindy giggled. "I'm an intern and I need to be fresh."

Kofi's eyes popped open. For the past few days, he'd been overcome with lust anytime she said she was an intern.

"You wanna play intern?" he asked with a wide grin. The sleep that had him in a chokehold loosened at the prospect of morning sex.

"No, baby. Be good."

Cindy lifted as Kofi watched from his elbow.

"You gotta shower," he insisted.

"Yes, but not the hour-long showers I have with you because you're fucking my brains out."

He stood. Every morning Cindy was enamored with the way his manhood greeted her at attention. Kofi's dick often beat him awake. She stared at him in the darkness. She'd been up long enough that her eyes had adjusted.

"I'm locking the door." Before she could turn, he used his long arms to his advantage and pulled her to him. "I'm nervous."

"About what? You know more than I did when I started."

"What if they have an issue with us being a couple?"

"We ain't a couple, baby. You about to be my wife."

Her body shuddered. She couldn't wait to marry Kofi. But what they had might not go over well at their place of work.

"Still, what's the policy on workplace relationships? Maybe Dr. Johns could put in a good word."

Kofi released her and waited until she faced him. "New rule, baby. Don't mention Johns when we're naked."

She giggled. "I'm not naked. You are."

"Everybody knows what time it is since you pulled your princess dress stunt. Ava covered for us as far as the loud fucking part, but she basically told everyone we made up."

"Oh."

Kofi found Cindy's neck and latched on. Just as he lifted her thin top over her head, his cellphone rang. He grabbed it and showed her that it was his mom.

"Hey, Ma," Kofi said. He tried to hide the irritation in his voice, but he hadn't fooled Cindy at all.

"Kofi Cornelius Carter," she started.

Cindy clapped her hands over her mouth. "Cornelius?" she whispered.

He nodded, then pinched her side. Her yelp was audible.

"I have a bone to pick with you too, Cynthia Miller," his mother added.

"Ma'am?"

"Why did I have to hear from Maurice that the two of you are getting married?"

"I'm sorry, Ma. I hadn't planned on proposing when I did. But when we made up it just felt right."

"Bring her to the house so we can all celebrate," his mother said. She sniffled, and her voice quivered as she spoke with a shaky voice.

"You OK, Ma?"

"My youngest child is getting married. I'm proud of you, Kofi."

"It's Cindy's first day as an intern. Can we stop by this week-end?" Kofi had his mother on speakerphone so they could both hear her clearly.

"I guess I don't have a choice, but if you come back for more clothes bring her with you. Don't keep slipping in and out of here."

"Yes, Ma'am."

Kofi disconnected the call and lifted Cindy. She didn't bother protesting because she wanted their shower ritual as much as he did.

* * *

Kofi had a harder time with the transition from home to work than Cindy. He couldn't keep his eyes off her thick frame as she bounced from room to room in her fitted scrubs.

"All of your taunting me about HR complaints, and you marry the first intern you see?" Johns boomed behind Kofi where he stood staring at her in conversation with another intern.

Although Johns still wasn't a fan of her initiative, she'd worn him down and won him over. As a result, Kofi's conversations with him were no longer as tense as they'd been when he started.

"I love her," Kofi admitted.

"Tell me something I don't know. It's obvious to anyone within a one-mile radius. She seems to be focused on the task at hand. I'm worried about you, though," Johns teased. He grabbed a notepad from the desk and moved around Kofi. "Pick up your jaw, Carter," Johns said as he moseyed away.

Kofi waved him off. Cindy was his woman. He'd waited years to have a chance with her, and the last one had been almost unbearable. Now that she had agreed to be his wife, he'd stare at her anytime he damn well pleased. Cindy gazed up and gave him a knowing smile. She leaned her head and motioned toward the back of the hospital.

He shot to his feet dropping a stack of papers when he did. *Does she mean what I think she means?* He pulled out his phone to make sure he wouldn't make a complete fool of himself.

Kofi: you flirting with me, Mrs. Carter?

Cindy pulled her phone from her back pocket while the other girl continued.

Future Mrs. Carter: I'm trying to let you see something. Think you can keep quiet?

He moaned. The other intern looked between them with a blush. Cindy said goodbye to her and headed to the back of the hospital without a second glance at Kofi. He berated himself for not keeping his cool. It was a shame how thirsty he was for this woman after he'd just had her a few hours earlier.

Kofi was so sprung there may as well had been stars where his eyes once were. Sex with her was amazing, but he loved other things about her just as deeply. He enjoyed the way she treated animals, and how committed she was to a cat who actually liked him better. He couldn't get enough of her voice, and the unselfish way she used it. It always put him in a better mood when Cindy sang, and she used it to her advantage on the few occasions when he was upset with her.

Kofi's heart sank when he thought about how Alonzo wouldn't walk her down the aisle. It was unfair that Cindy had to be without him because of her evil stepsister. Cindy had gotten to the point where it didn't trigger her to spend time with Dreeyah. Dreeyah was often at Kofi's parents' house when she and Dev visited. Kofi's dad was over the moon to have three additional women around. He loved his boys but was in heaven with the extra feminine energy.

Dreeyah teased Kofi about the confrontation they had the night of the ball when she thought he played Cindy for Stasia. It was a bittersweet memory they could now speak about without someone crying. Dreeyah confessed that she would have kicked his ass had her mom not held her back.

Kofi wore a goofy grin as he slowly picked up the papers he knocked over when his phone buzzed on the table where he set it.

It was a picture of a butt-naked Cindy with her panties rested on her pointer finger.

Future Mrs. Carter: Don't make me finish without you.

Kofi grabbed the stack of papers and used them to conceal his body's response to his favorite intern. He was the luckiest man in the world, and he couldn't be convinced otherwise.

Epilogue

Kofi officially moved out of his parents' home once Cindy said she'd marry him. He didn't need to stay the full year like he initially promised, because both Maurice and Dev got jobs. Dev got an apartment with Dreeyah, but Maurice still lived at home. Maurice said he wanted to save up for the house Ava deserved, and Norma was grateful all her boys weren't gone at once.

Stasia got twenty years in prison, while Detective Landry faced twenty-five years and two hundred and fifty thousand dollars in fines. Professor Brenton, Kofi, and her uncle David urged her not to worry herself with their punishments. When they were released, her loved ones would notify her, so she could rest easy in the meantime. It was a relief, and she was thankful for each one of them. Dreeyah didn't want anything to do with her mother or sister, and while Cindy understood, she suggested Dreeyah make peace with them, whether she stayed in contact or not.

Kofi couldn't help himself. He'd put an offer on a home while Cindy was at the hospital. She'd been there for several months and found a rhythm. She effortlessly rose above the few employees who didn't like her connection to Kofi. Although he wanted to confront each of them, she insisted it wasn't necessary because her work spoke for itself. Johns had also made her his protégé. He taught her as much as he could each day during her shift. Sometimes, she stayed late, like today.

"It's too big," Cindy groaned.

"No, it's not. You deserve it."

"Thank you, baby," she said as she stood in a hallway of four bedrooms. "The two of us need six rooms, Kofi?"

"Four bedrooms and two primary suites," he amended. His wide body leaned against the frame of a bedroom that had been painted pink. "Leena told me you were going to have four of my babies."

A few weeks ago, Felicia announced that she and Cindy's uncle David were expecting a son in the summer. Kofi had the nerve to be jealous. Cindy was thrilled to have a new aunt in Felicia. The two of them hadn't married, but Cindy still referred to her as Auntie. And when her uncle David said they were naming the baby Alonzo, Cindy was overcome with emotion.

Her first summer without her father would be rough, but with a namesake on the way, it would make the time of year that much sweeter. Cindy assured them that not only did she already love her cousin, but they had a built-in babysitter whenever they needed one.

She slapped Kofi's arm when something in the backyard caught her eye. "What are those?"

He smiled but said nothing.

"Kofi Carter, what are you up to now?"

She rushed down the stairs and out into the backyard. There were five bright red, freshly planted Japanese maples with bronzed garden plaques in front of them. They were engraved with the names of her parents, grandmothers, and her great aunt. When she turned to look at him, her eyes were filled with tears.

"Are you upset I did all this? Is it too much?" He bit his bottom lip, exposing his chipped tooth.

She shook her head. "This is the most thoughtful thing anyone has ever done for me. I love it, baby. And I love you, Kofi Carter."

He pulled her into him and hugged her like he'd die if he let go. "So this is love?" He sang off key. She snickered and nodded. "I love you too, Cynthia Miller Carter."

The End

In Real Life...

I write black love stories because I am an advocate for healthy love between black men and women. I seek to empower women to create the energy from my fictitious books in their real lives. After each of my titles, I'm going to feature real love stories. My first couple is Chaunte and Mike.

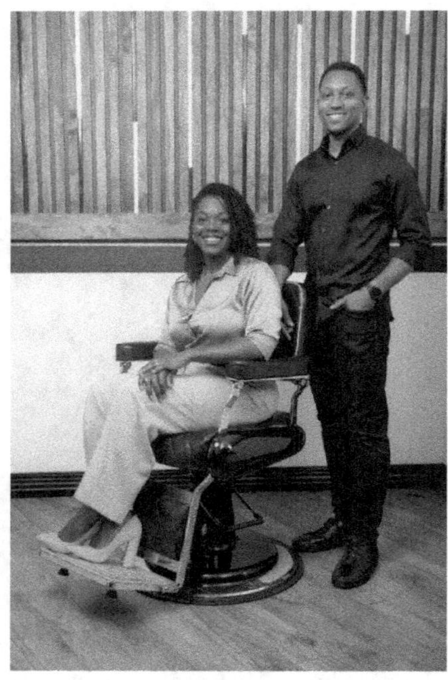

1. *Chaunte*, **how did you meet?**

Mike and I first crossed paths in high school in my ninth or tenth-grade year. Our deliberate connection, however, was solidified during my senior year near the oceanfront where we both lived. I spotted him down the beach. The details of how we connected are hazy, but I distinctly recall hanging out at his place shortly after.

When I ventured off to college we temporarily lost touch, but the magic of our bond lingered. One day while browsing Facebook, I spotted him online. I messaged him my number and added, "call me ASAP". Mike called immediately because he thought it was an emergency.

We've been inseparable since that phone call. Our journey has had its pauses and one significant break, but the underlying chemistry kept us connected.

1. ***Mike,* what is your favorite quality about your partner?**

For me, what stands out most about Chaunte is the radiant glow of her skin, especially in the early morning. I often find myself captivated by her beauty while she sleeps. Beyond that, I adore her sense of humor and wit which never fail to bring joy to our moments together.

1. ***Chaunte,* what is your pet peeve about your partner? (The thing that drives you nuts about them, but they are worth looking past it)**

The one quirk that occasionally drives me nuts about Mike is his tendency to leave cabinets and drawers wide open. He also forgets to close the refrigerator door. Despite these small annoyances, I overlook them because he's him, and his unique qualities make it all worth it.

1. ***Mike and Chaunte,*** what is your advice for people currently looking for love?

For women seeking healthy love, my advice is to be rooted in authenticity and self-awareness. Set both physical and mental boundaries that reflect your values and desires. Embrace the genuine connection you share with a potential partner, but don't be afraid to reclaim your time if something doesn't align. Healthy love exists beyond the pages of books and the frames of films when you prioritize self-love, maintain individuality, and communicate openly. It's about finding someone who appreciates you for who you are while encouraging your growth. ***-Chaunte***

My advice for people who desire genuine love beyond the pages of books or film is to avoid seeking completion in a partner. Instead, focus on personal healing for those aspects of yourself that need it. True fulfillment comes from within. *-Mike*

Thank you for finishing *Cindy Ella*.

If you enjoyed this story, **leave me a five-star rating and review on Amazon, and a positive review on Goodreads** and **TikTok.** And recommend it to your friends.

Also, I share freebies, sneak peeks, and discounts for sensual products on my mailing and SMS list! Sign up here.

http://eepurl.com/h15QoD
https://bit.ly/TextSweetHeat

Thank you in advance,
Denise Essex

Also by Denise Essex

More *Sweet Heat* Reads by Denise 💋

Daddy's Maybe
My Book

Prison Bae
https://bit.ly/PrisonBaeTrey

The Firemen's Ball: A Masquerade Affair
My Book

The Pleasure Package
https://bit.ly/pleasurepackage

A Naughty Rendezvous
https://bit.ly/ANaughtyRendezvous

Love in the same strip club
https://bit.ly/SameStripClub

Heat Haven Heaux-Tell: Three Novellas
https://bit.ly/HeatHaven

The College Route
https://bit.ly/TheCollegeRoute

I Found Her

https://amzn.to/3VmWLm7

The Visiting Professor

https://bit.ly/TheVisitingProfessor

Gone For a Soldier

https://bit.ly/GoneForASoldier

Let's Connect!

Where to find me in these intanet streets 💋

TikTok: tiktok.com/@deniseessex222 **(Help me reach 1K by New Year's Day** 🎉 **)**
Amazon Author Page: https://www.amazon.com/author/denise_essex
Readers Group:
https://www.facebook.com/groups/deniseessexheatseekers

Facebook page: https://www.facebook.com/DeniseEssexAuthor
INSTAGRAM: https://www.instagram.com/deniseessex222/
IG Handle: @DeniseEssex222
TikTok: @DeniseEssex222
Twitter: @DeniseEssex222

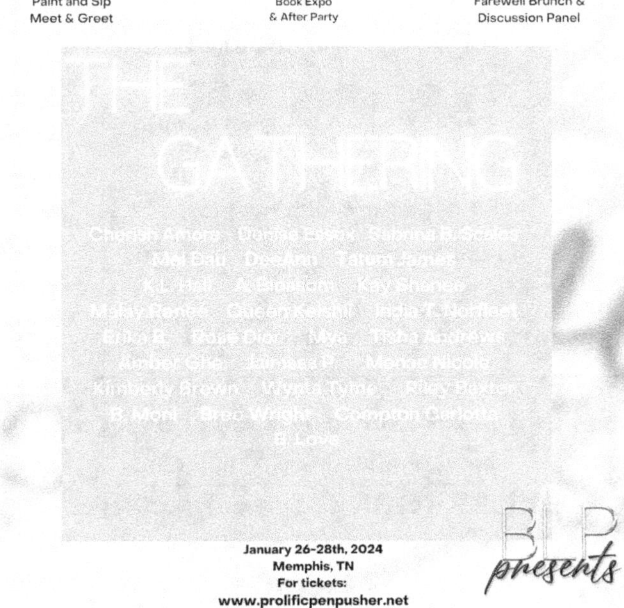

What a time to be a Black girl who loves books!
January 26th-28th, 2024
Memphis, TN
Featuring: The Authors of BLP
Hosted by: B. Love

To register, click here - https://www.prolificpenpusher. net/blp-the-gathering

Visit bit.ly/readBLP to join our mailing list for sneak peeks and release day links!

B. Love Publications - where Authors celebrate black men, black women, and black love.
To submit a manuscript for consideration, email your first three chapters to blovepublications@gmail.com with SUBMISSION as the subject.

The BLP Podcast – bit.ly/BLPUncovered

Let's connect on social media!
Facebook - B. Love Publications
Twitter - @blovepub
Instagram - @blovepublications

We hate errors, but we are human! If the B. Love team leaves any grammatical errors behind, do us a kindness and send them to us directly in an email to blovepublications@gmail.com **with ERRORS as the subject line.**

As always, if you enjoyed this book, please leave a review on Amazon/Goodreads, recommend it on social media and/or to a friend, and mark it as READ on your Goodreads profile.